The Winds of Summer

The
WINDS
of
SUMMER

by David Roth

Criterion Books
Published by Abelard-Schuman Limited
London   New York   Toronto

F
R845W

For my parents
and for Lucy

12,126
11-73
4.95

Criterion Books are published by Abelard-Schuman Ltd.
Published on the same day in Canada by Abelard-Schuman Canada Limited

LONDON	NEW YORK	TORONTO
Abelard-Schuman	Abelard-Schuman	Abelard-Schuman
Limited	Limited	Canada Limited
8 King St.	257 Park Ave. So.	228 Yorkland Blvd.
WC2	10010	425

An **Intext** Publisher

Printed in the United States of America

Contents

ONE

~~~~~~~~~~~~~~~~~~~~~~~~~~~~~~~~

The *Wild Wind*

He and Granddad hauled along the east side of Hunter Island, picking up a load of traps on the way down the shore to shift out onto the Triangle Ground. They took on board only twenty traps from all those they hauled, but by the time they finished setting these traps in pairs on long warps, it was midafternoon on the Triangle Ground, the June sun slanting into their eyes from the west. In the distance Hunter Island lay low on the water, a green and gray line except for the broad stone hump of Alder Mountain. On the way in to sell, Petey Shannon washed down the *Jenny and Susan* before pulling off his oil pants and sitting on a crate in the stern of the boat.

His red sweatshirt fluttered around his thin frame in the wind that swept by the sides of the deckhouse. The wind was working on his salty black hair too, and he locked his hands over his head, fighting a headache. Up forward in the stinking heat under the deckhouse roof Granddad Will was standing by the wheel, keeping the boat on her course toward town. Petey noticed how tired he looked each time the old man turned his way. But at

7

fifteen Petey was still young enough to avoid doing some of the things he knew he should do.

Finally Granddad motioned him to take the wheel. Petey exchanged places with him, then cut their speed as they entered the narrows between Cemetery Point and Mussel Island. Behind him Granddad was checking their catch of lobsters.

"Maybe a hundred pounds," Granddad called. "Not bad."

Petey hardly heard him, for he had already spotted another boat, the *Wild Wind,* up ahead. She was a bright, moving shape at the far end of Mussel Island, growing larger as the distance closed between them. Granddad came forward to take the wheel again, and they both watched her approach, Petey with the empty feeling inside he got every time he saw her.

"Deven must be playing around," Granddad said. "No bodies for him today."

The *Wild Wind* slowed down to pass them on their port side. She was a twenty-eight-foot powerboat, smaller than the *Jenny and Susan,* but her graceful lines gave her a look of flowing life Granddad's boat lacked. Petey raised his hand halfheartedly to Mr. Deven who jumped back from the wheel to wave both arms at them. His bald head shone in the hard sunlight.

"Been celebrating, I'd guess," Granddad growled. "Probably heard someone was sick."

Petey said nothing. He watched the *Wild Wind* slide away, picking up speed as she left them. The undertaker long ago had painted her different colors and removed her hauling gear, but she still looked like the lobster boat

Dad had built. She still moved on the water, in the wind and chop, the way she had moved beneath Dad's feet and his. . . .

"I know," Granddad said, guessing his thoughts. "Every time I think of the way Deven made me give him that boat, I could throw my boots overboard. If he had just allowed us time, we could have paid him off. But he was bound to have the *Wild Wind.*"

"Let's drop it," Petey said. His father had built the *Wild Wind* himself, but when he died Mr. Deven had forced Granddad to give the boat to him as payment for the funeral. During that fateful summer when Petey was nine, he had hauled with Dad on the *Wild Wind*, and his memories of those last days with Dad were tied to memories of their boat, strong and alive beneath them. Each time he saw her now, she brought back to him a sense of all he had lost.

When they came into the harbor, Granddad guided the *Jenny and Susan* in beside Carl Julian's lobster car. Petey tied up with a half hitch over the winch head.

"How'd you hit them today?" Julian asked. He was a tall, stocky man with a voice that boomed out of him as if his chest was hollow.

"Numb, I call them," Granddad said. He and Petey lifted their barrel up to the washboard. As Julian tip-rolled it to the scales, Petey followed him with the bushel basket containing the rest of their lobsters.

"How's the littlest Shannon?" Julian teased, taking the basket from Petey.

When Petey turned away without answering, Granddad told Julian about seeing the *Wild Wind* on their way in. "The boy still thinks the world of that boat. Always will, I guess."

Julian had placed the bushel basket on top of the barrel on the scales. He took out his pad, adjusted the weights and wrote down the total. "Well, I hear tell Deven wants to get rid of her."

Petey watched Julian drop the lobsters into one of the underwater compartments within the car through an opening in the planks. The buyer's words had snapped him out of his dark mood.

"That the truth?" he asked.

"That's the word around the harbor." Julian turned toward Granddad as he weighed the empty barrel and basket. "Any bait?"

"Better give us four bushels of brim and a bushel of herring."

Petey forked the bright red brim into their bait barrels, then shoveled the slippery herring into the bushel basket. When Granddad went up to the office with Julian to get their money, Petey filled another basket full of brim and kicked it under the stern. Granddad expected him to do this to help make up for the amount Julian cheated them on the weight of their catch, but he felt guilty just the same. He was busy covering the bait with salt when Julian and Granddad returned down the ladder.

"What's the price?" he asked Granddad as they eased away from the car.

"The same. Fifty-five cents."

"How many pounds?"

"Ninety-one."

"We had more than that. I think we should go across and sell in Grant Harbor."

Granddad snorted. "Time you figure in your extra gas to the mainland, you're not making a cent more."

They were threading their way carefully through the boats on their moorings. "You suppose Julian is telling the truth?" Petey asked.

"About what?"

"About Mr. Deven selling the *Wild Wind.*"

"First I've heard of it. I wouldn't believe anything Julian told me."

"Yeah, but . . ."

"Wouldn't be nothing we could do about it, even if Deven is selling," Granddad snapped. He brought the boat in beside Mel Swift's float.

While they gassed up, Petey finished washing down the platform. He was deep in his thoughts when Granddad handed him a ten-dollar bill. "Go up and pay and get a couple quarts of oil."

Petey crossed the float and bounded up the ramp. When he came out of the garage with the oil, he saw Uncle Leo driving in beside the air hose.

Leo climbed out of his pickup. "How'd you hit them, Petey?"

"Not so hot." Petey watched him putting air in a nearly flat back tire. "Why don't you fix that?"

"No need to yet." Leo looked up at Petey. The sun was full on his sweating face which was tanned and lined beneath bristly brown hair. "I pump it up when I get to town and then once or twice before I start for home. Okay with you?"

Petey nodded. "How's business?"

Leo laughed. He coiled up the air hose and returned to the pickup. "I'll never get rich this way." He ground gears going into reverse. Petey watched him drive away on the wrong side of the street, garbage spilling out over the plywood sides of his truck.

Petey jumped down the ramp and handed Granddad the oil and the change from the ten-dollar bill. "Leo's been drinking again."

"Why tell me about it?"

Petey sometimes thought Granddad aged five years during a hard day on the water. It was a kind of aging that went beyond his gray hair and leathery brown face. And now, at the mention of Leo, even his massive shoulders sagged.

Petey turned away to cast off the line.

"One son dead, the other a seasick no-good, hellbent on becoming an alcoholic before he's thirty." Granddad cursed. "Shove her off there, Petey! Let's head for home."

They cut out into the wind toward the mouth of the harbor. "After expenses, your share comes to seven dollars," Granddad told him, handing him the bills. Petey pocketed the money. They rolled in the chop as Granddad turned the bow.

Beyond the harbor the slanting sun glared off the water. Petey looked for the *Wild Wind*, but she wasn't yet on her way in.

TWO

~~~~~~~~~~~~~~~~~~~~~~~~~~~~~~~~

The Return of Spider Tate

As they came around the high rock face of Tragedy Bluff into East Bay, all the familiar marks of home seemed magnified in the glowing light from a western cloud bank. Gulls circled and wove above the low rock and sand line of Seal Bar which formed the northern arm of the bay. When they turned in toward Rocky Point, Petey went to the side to watch Parsons Ledge slide by. Just as they entered Fox Cove, the sun came out of the clouds, casting long shadows from the spruce trees above the rocks.

The engine roared in reverse as Petey hurried out onto the bow to gaff the mooring buoy from out of the punt. When the mooring pennant was secure and Granddad had killed the engine, Petey stood there on the bow, listening to the silence, until Granddad yelled at him to come aft with the punt.

Petey rowed them to shore. There was a small outboard motor on the stern of the punt, but he didn't bother to start it. While he was tying the punt on the pulley line, Granddad scrambled up the rocks to the

path that ran along one side of Fox Cove through
the wild grass.

"You want supper or don't you?" he called.

"Been a long time since morning," Petey said as they
walked in long strides toward the house.

Granddad grunted in agreement.

Before supper Petey went up to his room to change
into dry clothes. From his window he could look out over
Fox Cove to where the *Jenny and Susan* floated at her
mooring. He liked the evenings after a long haul when
the deep tiredness settled into every part of his body
and he could lie on his bed looking out the window,
drifting. . . .

Gram called him to come eat. Before he went down,
he took his money hoard of thirteen dollars from the top
drawer of his bureau and put it in his wallet with the
seven dollars he had made that day. The picture of his
mother on the bureau stared at him with disapproval, as
if she knew what he was doing.

Downstairs, Gram Jenny, small, thin and gray, was
scurrying around the kitchen serving supper. Petey took
his seat opposite Granddad at the round table. Leo
wasn't home yet, but he was often late getting back from
his garbage route.

"Going to town tonight?" Granddad asked him.

Petey chewed on a tough piece of pot roast. "Yes sir."

Granddad nodded. "Money sure burns a hole in your
pocket when you're fifteen."

"He's going to put his money right into the bank and

save it toward college," Gram said. Her thin hands gripped the vegetable dish tightly as she moved it next to Petey's plate.

"No, I can't."

"Petey!"

He tried to match her stare, but her eyes were too sharp. Years ago he remembered her as a woman who laughed kindly at everything, especially when laughter was needed. Dad's death had changed this, and the years since, with the lobstering getting a little poorer all the time, hadn't helped. And then there was Leo, late again.

She turned now to Granddad. "Will, can't you make him mind?"

Granddad studied the patterns in his gravy. "The boy works hard, Jenny. He buys all his own clothes, pays his board. He can spend the rest of his money any way he sees fit."

"That's what I thought you'd say."

They were still fighting when Petey went to the entry for his jacket. Granddad had lit his corncob pipe and was looking at the Sears, Roebuck catalog, surrounded by a cloud of smoke.

"You be home by eleven, you hear?" Gram called to Petey as he slammed out through the side door.

He walked around Granddad's car and crossed the dusty dooryard. The sun was going down near Alder Mountain, the highest ridge on Hunter Island. Crows were calling in the spruce woods over on Rocky Point, their cries cutting into the silence, making it seem deeper. Petey could hear the Tates' dog Killer barking on the other side of the ridge.

It was five miles to town, but he was used to going down on foot. He trotted the half mile to the main road and walked on as long as the way was uphill. At the crest he came out of the woods momentarily, then raced down Alder Mountain Hill into the deep shadows under Dead Man's Cliff. When he came out again into the open, he imagined his feet were barely touching the hard dirt beneath him.

He was up to the fork in the road by the Tates' mailbox before he stopped running. Beyond the sound of his own hard breathing, he heard a truck spinning through gravel on the Tates' road. He jumped for the cover of the bushes.

From behind a screen of young fir trees he watched the Tates' pickup truck lurch over the last rise and swing onto the main road where it backfired and stalled. In the sudden silence the grinding starter sounded weak, fading fast. Petey crouched as low as he could. He didn't want to be seen, for Spider Tate had returned from prison only last week. Petey didn't feel ready to face him.

The dog Killer began to growl and jumped from the body of the pickup just as the engine came chugging back to life.

One of the doors snapped open. "Get over here, Killer!"

Petey backed quickly into the woods, but it was too late. The Tates' old mongrel had picked up his scent and was charging toward him through the bushes. The rough bark of a large tree slammed against Petey's back. He broke off a dead branch from above and held it close so that he would be able to swing it down quickly. Killer shot through into the clear and began to circle to Petey's left. His growling grew louder and deeper.

"Get back, Killer!" Spider shouted hoarsely as he forced his way through the undergrowth. "I wouldn't use that club if I was you, boy."

"Then call off your mangy dog." Petey stared at Spider's grinning, unshaven face, at the heavy, cruel features he had remembered and hated for so long. Spider hadn't changed much in prison. He was a little thinner, a little more gaunt, his crouch a bit more like an animal's in its menace.

"Who is it?" Danny Tate called from the road. His voice was higher than Spider's, more of a cracking whine. Killer began to growl again.

Spider laughed. "Killer here has cornered himself a Shannon."

Danny crashed through the bushes, giggling as he came. He was a smaller, homelier copy of Spider, with a narrow head and enormous eyes. Petey tried to move away to the right.

"Hold it there, boy," Spider shouted. "Where're you bound for this fine evening?"

"I'm going to town."

"So are we. Down to the Half Tide to shoot some pool. You might as well ride along with us."

"I'll walk."

Spider laughed again. "Hear that, Danny? The boy don't seem to want to ride with us." Spider stepped closer. "What's the matter, boy? Ain't you glad to see me home?"

"I knew you were back."

"But you ain't happy to see me?"

Petey shook his head.

Danny slipped over and grabbed Petey's right arm with his clawlike fingers. "He's coming with us, ain't he, Spider? Ain't he coming with us?"

"That's right. We got to talk to this boy. Take him up to the truck and don't let him get away from you."

On the ride to town Petey had to sit between them, and the whisky smell of their breath made him sick. Danny's driving took them all over the road.

"Let me sit next to the door," Petey shouted at Spider. "I want to be able to jump when your brother ditches this wreck."

"Shut up," Danny snarled. "Spider has something to tell you."

"What?"

"We saw you and your grandfather take a load of traps out to the Triangle Ground today," Spider said thickly. He paused to light a cigarette.

"We can set traps where we please," Petey told him.

As the cab of the truck filled with smoke, Danny began coughing, bowing his head over the steering wheel. At the last moment he pulled the truck away from the edge of the road.

"You listen to me good, boy," Spider said. "Now that I'm home here with Danny, we mean to get back what's ours. The Triangle Ground belongs to us. You tell your grandfather to keep his traps off that bottom!"

"The Triangle Ground isn't yours!"

"Our old man drowned out there. That was before you

was even born. He set more gear on the Triangle Ground than any other lobsterman in his time. He paid for that bottom with the traps he lost, then with his life. You understand me, boy? It's ours, bought and paid for!"

Spider was shouting. He grabbed Petey's jacket and shook him savagely. "If you don't get off the Triangle Ground," he raged, "I'll take care of you and Gramps the way I took care of your father."

Petey hit him in the face. Spider's sharp whiskers scraped against his fist. Spider knocked his arm away and punched him in the stomach. Before they reached town, he opened his door.

"Stop here," he ordered Danny. "Okay, Shannon, you've been warned. Now we begin playing rough. You want to save your hide, you better get on the mainland and stay with your Mom."

Spider pushed him out of the truck onto the road. Petey watched them drive off toward Main Street, his stomach aching so hard he couldn't breathe without sobbing. When they were gone, it seemed as if he could still hear Spider's ugly voice.

THREE

~~~~~~

The Price of a Dream

Petey could remember clearly the night his father died. He remembered waking up and hearing Mom crying. He had crept down to find out what was wrong, and in the darkness of the stairs heard two men from town trying to quiet Mom, heard Canada, Dad's best friend, erupt into a crying fit that was half rage, half tenderness. Shivering in the chilly darkness he had moved quietly to the foot of the stairs to look through the dimly lighted living room into the kitchen. There it hit him that Dad, his own wild, strong, impossible-to-keep-up-with father had died—in a fight with Spider Tate.

And then, before the funeral, when he saw the body in the coffin, it wasn't Dad at all, just a clay dummy that made Petey turn away, swallowing his nausea. The undertaker, Mr. Deven, asked him how he thought his father looked. Petey ran outside without answering him.

Through it all beat two words, like two drums alternately pounding: Spider Tate, Spider Tate. He had killed Dad, he was in jail, he would be punished; but Petey dreamed a hundred dreams of revenge until he couldn't sleep at night.

Through the funeral in the church in town, through the burial itself in the little cemetery near Fox Cove, the drumbeat of that hated name went on and on.

And now Spider was back after the years in prison for killing Dad. He was back on Hunter Island, back on the water with his brother Danny and threatening to start a fight over the Triangle Ground. . . .

Petey had walked right past Mr. Deven's house. He doubled back, forcing away thoughts that didn't want to leave him alone. Mrs. Deven told him her husband wasn't home.

"I think you'll find him down to his wharf," she added. "He said something about grounding out his boat to-night."

He thanked her and returned to the street. The door didn't close immediately behind him and he knew she was watching him go, wondering what he wanted with her husband.

As Petey walked along Main Street, he kept watch for Uncle Leo. The town was quiet even this early in the evening. At the bottom of Signal Hill where Shallow Harbor Road intersected Main Street he crossed over to the water-front side.

Canada was sitting on one of the benches in front of the Half Tide Pool Room. Through the wide screen door behind him the sounds of clicking balls punctuated the shouts and laughter of the men inside. The Tates' pickup was pulled in at the curb, and Killer growled from the body as Petey walked closer.

"Hey Petey," Canada called. "Let's have a game of points."

Petey shook his head. "Can't tonight. I got something to do."

Canada smiled his easy smile. "Don't let the Tates scare you off. Come on."

"Have you seen Leo around?" Petey asked. He didn't want to talk about the Tates. What they had done to him on the ride to town was a private thing.

Canada stood up and stretched. He was only a little taller than Petey, but much heavier and stronger from a lifetime of cutting wood and hauling traps. There was a scar running the length of his face, from forehead to chin on the left side.

"Leo was here about an hour ago," Canada told him. "Played a few hands of stud in the back room, then left."

Petey nodded. "It's just I'm hoping to ride home with him."

Canada's face glowed darkly in the fading evening light. "He was feeling no pain when I saw him, Petey. Maybe you'll be better off walking."

"Yeah, well, I'll see you around."

"Come in the poolroom sometime. I'll give you a few pointers on your play so you can take on Spider."

"I will."

Petey walked on toward Mr. Deven's wharf. The wind from the afternoon was dying now, but it still shook the weeds that grew next to the sidewalk and moaned in the telephone wires overhead. In the deep sky glow and the cool wind the loneliness of the sea was very strong.

As he left the main part of town behind him, he heard an engine roaring in reverse. Petey jumped a ditch and ran by a shed to the end of Mr. Deven's private wharf, where he caught the stern line Mr. Deven tossed to him from the *Wild Wind*. He tied it around the top of a spile, then went to take the bowline.

"Thank you," Mr. Deven called. He adjusted the slack on both lines to allow for the lowering of the boat with the tide, then lifted a board in the *Wild Wind*'s platform and began pumping bilge water into a bucket with a hand pump.

"Leak?" Petey asked.

"Seems to be taking on more than usual," Mr. Deven said.

Petey slipped over the edge of the wharf and swung down onto the washboard. It had been a long time since he had last come on board the *Wild Wind*, and he looked around eagerly in the twilight to see what had been changed. Mr. Deven stopped pumping to watch him.

"You've always thought a lot about this old boat, haven't you, Petey?"

"Yes sir, but she isn't old."

"Your father built her three years before he passed away, didn't he?"

"Yeah, but that doesn't make her old." Petey took a deep breath. "I hear you're thinking of selling her."

"It might be I am, Petey."

"Well, I heard you were and I wanted to get in on it before someone else . . ." His voice trailed off weakly. Mr. Deven was laughing.

"You mean you want to buy her?"

"Sure I do." Petey couldn't see what was so funny. "I mean, I couldn't pay you all at once, but . . ."

"Well, I'll tell you the way it is," Mr. Deven said. "I'm

going to sell her, but not until this fall. I want something that's more of a party boat with a head and a galley and the works. But I'm not buying until after the summer people leave and prices go down to normal. In the meantime, I'll be keeping the *Wild Wind*."

Petey felt the extra time gave him a better chance. He was nearly sick with eagerness. "How much do you want for her?"

"Oh, I'd have to get five hundred dollars," Mr. Deven said. He picked up the bilge bucket and emptied it over the side. "Five hundred at the very least."

Petey shook his head with disappointment. "That's a lot of money."

"Not really. This is a good boat."

"She's nine years old."

"You told me yourself she isn't old." Mr. Deven leaned over to light a cigarette. Petey stared at the long, tapering fingers that held the flickering match.

"She leaks," he said lamely.

"A good caulking all over would take care of that." Mr. Deven began slowly pumping again.

Petey walked to the stern and looked out at the lights across the harbor. He knew how badly he wanted the *Wild Wind*. Despite the way she leaked she was basically sound—all she needed was to be hauled up this coming winter for a thorough working over in the spring. In the meantime the worst leaks could be stopped by grounding her out and caulking the seams that needed it most. He wanted her and she was his by rights—he had always felt that this was true. But five hundred dollars. How would he save up that much?

Mr. Deven asked him to go up onto the wharf and turn on the lights. Petey went up and opened the door to the shed and found the switch. When he flicked it down, the wharf was bathed in the weak light from three overhead bulbs. He could see Mr. Deven bent over his pumping below him.

"I've made up my mind," Petey called down to him. "I'll pay your price."

Mr. Deven watched him climb down into the boat. "Listen, Petey . . ."

"You really want to sell her this fall, don't you?"

"Yes, I'm definitely going to sell."

"I want to buy her. I know five hundred dollars is a lot of money, but I can raise most of it hauling with Granddad, and I'll get the rest somehow between now and the end of summer."

"Petey, to tell you the truth . . ."

Petey waited, but Mr. Deven stopped himself. He walked to the side and began pulling down rocks and placing them on the washboard to keep the boat leaning in against the wharf as the tide left her.

"Don't you want to sell her to me?" Petey asked.

"I don't think you can pay the price."

"But I'll be working real hard this summer."

"I can't wait forever while you try to raise the money. I'll need ready cash for the boat I'll be buying." Mr. Deven moved a small barrel next to the washboard and filled it with buckets of water. "There, that should do it, don't you think, Petey? She's got a good list."

"Yes sir, plenty." Petey plunged ahead. "Suppose I give you some money now, like a down payment, and then I could pay you the rest in the fall."

"How much do you have?"

Petey reached into his back pocket and squeezed his wallet. "Twenty dollars."

"That's not much of a down payment."

Petey felt his chance slipping away. "When exactly did you have in mind to sell the *Wild Wind?*"

"September."

"Suppose I give you this twenty dollars now and the rest of the five hundred whenever you say?"

"I don't know."

"Look, if I can't raise the rest, you can keep my down payment." Petey tried to catch his breath. He knew he wasn't bargaining well—he was too excited. All that mattered was getting the *Wild Wind.* "You can't be hurt," he went on. "Either I pay you the rest of the money when you want it or I lose my twenty dollars and you can sell to someone else."

"What you want is an option, first refusal."

"Yes sir, if that means I get first chance to buy her."

"Okay, Petey. I'll take your down payment. But your deadline will be the first day of September. After that I'll be free to sell elsewhere."

"Yes sir." Petey dug out his wallet and handed the twenty dollars to Mr. Deven.

"You wait a moment and I'll make you out a receipt." Mr. Deven crawled forward into the bow and pulled on a light. When he came back a couple of minutes later, he handed Petey a small piece of paper torn from a grocery bag. Petey held it up to the light from the wharf, but he couldn't read the writing.

"It says that on this day I received twenty dollars from you as down payment on the *Wild Wind*, the balance of four hundred and eighty dollars to be paid by noon on September first. Fair enough?"

"Yes sir." Petey put the receipt into his wallet.

"Tell you the truth, Petey, I don't think you'll be able to get the money. You only have a little over two months."

"I'll get it," Petey said firmly.

"If you say so." Mr. Deven climbed onto the washboard. "I'm going home. Coming?"

"Would you let me take her out, just to check her over?"

"I'll be finished working on her before high water tomorrow afternoon. Come down then."

"If I can," Petey said. "I'll meet you after five. The tide should be high enough to float her by then."

"All right." Mr. Deven turned off the lights and locked the shed door. "Good night."

"See you," Petey called.

He waited until Mr. Deven had driven off in his car. Then he climbed up to sit on the edge of the wharf. It was full night now, but he could see the outline of the *Wild Wind* below him. He wanted to be near her for a while, now that she was going to be his.

As he sat there in the darkness listening to the sounds that drifted over the harbor, he slipped away into another day when the platform of the *Wild Wind* would roll beneath his feet as the sea ran under and the sky looked down, a thousand miles high.

FOUR

~~~~~~

Wrecking One Truck

When he started back through town, he was still hoping to find Leo. He hurried along the sidewalk. It was later than he had realized, for the Half Tide Pool Room was closed.

"Wait up, Petey."

He turned to see Sheila Wilson behind him. "Where did you come from?"

She walked up to him and turned his face toward the street light above the poolroom. "There. Now I can read your lips."

He felt himself begin to blush. "I said I didn't know you were around."

"I saw you down at Mr. Deven's wharf. You didn't see me because I didn't want you to."

Petey struggled for something more to say. He didn't know Sheila well, because she was a year older and because she was deaf and kept to herself.

"Why were you sitting on Mr. Deven's wharf?" she asked. She spoke quickly and softly, running her words together so that it was hard for Petey to understand her.

"I'm going to buy the *Wild Wind* back from him."

28

"Really?"

He nodded. "This fall I'll be setting my own gear, hauling afternoons and weekends."

"Will your grandfather let you?"

"He'll let me," Petey insisted before he realized she was teasing him. He had let his excitement show, and she was making him feel like a little boy. During the pause in their conversation he became aware of the distant generator hum from the power plant. Main Street was empty, still and lifeless.

Sheila took off her scarf and tossed back her long black hair.

"What are you doing out so late?" he asked.

"Just walking. My sisters don't care. Why should you?"

"I don't." He licked his dry lips. Sheila's face moved closer to his as she watched his mouth. "I just wondered why you were alone, that's all. I thought Wilbur Hartwell was your boyfriend."

"He's not really my boyfriend." She took his hand. The street light hung above them like a huge star, glaring down upon the pavement. "Walk with me? We have the whole night to ourselves."

He held back. "I can't. I have to get home."

"What?"

"I can't."

She released his hand. "Okay. Good night, Petey."

She crossed the street to the sidewalk in front of the parking lot. He started to go after her, but realized what he was doing and stopped. When she turned up Shallow Harbor Road, he felt suddenly alone.

Petey headed for Fox Cove along East Bay Road, running part of the time and walking when he had to catch his breath. Clouds were covering the sky, and a new breeze smelling of fog stirred the leaves on the birch trees. In the darkness he didn't see Uncle Leo's pickup until he was nearly beside it.

"Hey Leo," he called.

No answer came back to him. The truck was parked at the edge of the ditch. Petey wrenched open the door on the driver's side and found Leo sprawled over on the seat.

"Wake up, Leo," Petey shouted. He grabbed one of Leo's arms and shook him hard. Somewhere on the seat, a cache of empty beer cans clattered together before rolling onto the floor.

"Come on, Leo. You can't sleep here all night."

Leo pulled himself up straight and swung his head around in the darkness. "Who's there?"

The fright in Leo's voice surprised Petey. "Just me, Leo. Who were you expecting?"

"Oh." Leo shook himself and stretched as much as he could in the truck. "Want a ride home?"

"Yeah. Can you drive?"

Leo slid over onto the other side of the seat. "You drive. I've got another beer here somewhere." As Petey climbed in behind the wheel, Leo flipped through the pile of beer cans on the floor looking for the full one. Petey heard the can hiss as Leo opened it.

"Go easy on the way home," Leo told him. "That tail pipe's about had it."

Petey started the engine and pulled on the lights. As

they rolled along the rough road, he took a deep breath. He had never driven before at night. The right headlight raked the trees beside the road. The left light bore down on the dirt only a few feet ahead. But Petey could see the dim outline of the road beyond, and he followed it up and down the sharp, short hills and around the twisting curves.

As he drove through the night, his thoughts returned to the *Wild Wind*. He would tell Leo later. He would surprise him along with Gram and Granddad.

"I'm about ruined, Petey," Leo said suddenly. Petey glanced around as Leo drank from his can of beer.

"What's the matter?"

"They won't pay me." He swore and rolled up his window. It jammed halfway. "I keep hauling away all the garbage they come up with, week after week, and are they grateful? No sir. Fifty cents a week, but can they pay me? No sir. Widow Moore owes me ten dollars and fifty cents."

"Quit on her."

"Sure. Know what I made today?"

Petey slowed down for a stretch of washboard he thought he saw in the road ahead. "How much?"

Leo reached into his back pocket and brought out a moneybag. He dumped the change into one hand and peered at it carefully in the light from the dashboard. "Two dollars and seventeen cents."

"Yeah, but how about all this beer you've been drinking?"

"The garbageman is low man on the totem pole," Leo went on, "the man at the bottom of the heap of life. But if it wasn't for us, the whole world would choke on its own leavings. Think about it, Petey."

"I will."

As they chugged up Alder Mountain Hill, Leo finished his beer and dropped the empty can among the others at his feet. Petey cut around the curve at the top of the hill, and they headed down the long slope on the other side. On the way down, the headlights flared momentarily, then died. The oncoming road became a blur. Petey worked the switch in and out, but nothing happened.

"Burned out a fuse or something," Leo said. "Better see if you can slow this thing down, Petey."

Petey tried to guess how close they were to the ditch, for as he hit the brakes, the truck lurched to the right, skidding on the dirt. He let up on the brakes a moment. When he pressed the pedal down again, it shot to the floor. He pumped on the brakes uselessly. There was no returning pressure.

"Why don't you slow down?" Leo asked peevishly.

"I can't. The brakes just let go." Petey wrestled with the wheel as they went from one side of the road to the other, but hard as he tried, he couldn't straighten out. Every few seconds he caught a glimpse of trees flying past them.

"Hang on!" Leo yelled. "There's a big hump along here somewhere."

"I'm trying!" Petey yelled back. It made him feel better to shout.

When they hit the high place in the road, Petey bounced and rapped his head on the roof. The steering wheel spun out of his hands, wrenching one of his thumbs. Somewhere in his mind he noticed that the engine was making more noise.

"There! You lost the muffler."

Petey had a new grip on the wheel, but it was too late. A dark cloud of branches rushed over the windshield. The pickup bounced right, then left. Leo was swearing at the top of his voice.

Petey thought they were going to flip over, but then, instead, they hit something head-on and jolted to a stop.

Leo was breathing much too loudly. It was several moments before Petey smelled the steam and realized the radiator had ruptured, spraying water all over the hot engine.

"You okay?" Leo asked.

Petey felt the top of his head. "I think so."

"Why didn't you try shifting down?"

"I didn't think of it," Petey admitted.

"That's what I thought. Want to sit here a while?"

"Not especially."

Leo's door opened with a loud snap. They slid onto the ground and walked around the truck, surveying the damage with the help of Leo's cigarette lighter. The pickup had come to rest against a large boulder at the edge of a field near their own road. The right front fender was wrapped tightly around the tire. The hood had been sprung, and the impact of the crash had driven the radiator back against the engine. On their second walk around Petey saw that one side of the plywood body had been torn off during their passage through the trees.

"Guess we were lucky." Petey shivered in the chill night air. "I'm sorry, Leo."

"We're both alive," Leo said. "Let's call that good enough."

They had walked halfway home when Leo began to laugh. The sound of his voice echoed loudly in the dark and starless night.

~~~~~~~~~~~~~~~~~~~~~~~~~~~~~~~

FIVE

And Buying Another

When Petey woke up, it was later than usual. He rolled over and saw the solid gray fog through the window. They wouldn't haul today. He thought about going back to sleep, but in the end he decided to get dressed. He had to tell them about the *Wild Wind*.

Leo was already up, sitting at the kitchen table hunched over a cup of coffee, with a cigarette burning untended in a nearby ash tray. "Well, here comes next year's winner of the Indianapolis Five Hundred."

"It's your own fault for letting him drive," Granddad said. He was knitting trap heads in the corner near the doorway to the front room. As he looked across at Petey, the long wooden needle in his hand hardly slowed.

Gram slammed the lid down on the stove. "Wonder is they weren't both killed."

"It's all a matter of being relaxed, Mom," Leo said. He knocked the ash from his cigarette and brought the end to his mouth. "I was real loose and Petey was enjoying himself."

"Go ahead and joke about it," Gram said. "You

never had any sense. A man twenty-eight carrying on like a boy."

"Yes ma'am."

"Just don't lead Petey down the same path you're traveling, that's all."

"I have no intention of doing that."

Gram dropped three pieces of bacon into her black frying pan. The hiss they made as they fried filled out a long silence. "I hope you mean it, Leo," she said.

Leo winked at Petey. "Fact is, I never saw a sign of him all evening until we got together on the way home."

Petey filled his coffee cup and slipped into his chair.

"Did you spend all your money, Petey?" Gram demanded.

"Yes, I did, but . . ."

"On what?" Leo asked. "Sheila Wilson was hanging around town yesterday. You don't suppose she latched onto him, do you?"

Petey pretended to find a new design in the pattern of the tablecloth. He felt his face turning red.

"Stop laughing like that," Gram snapped at Leo. "Petey wouldn't have anything to do with a girl like Sheila Wilson." She took Petey's plate and filled it with bacon and two pieces of toast. "Petey, why did you stay down street so late?"

"I'm going to buy the *Wild Wind*," Petey told them angrily. Leo had spoiled everything. He hadn't gone walking with Sheila. Besides, the news about the boat was the only important thing, and now his whole surprise was ruined.

"How are you going to do that?" Granddad asked.

Petey explained quickly. When he was finished, there

wasn't a convinced face among them.

"Five hundred dollars!" Granddad snorted. "She ain't worth that anymore."

"She is to me," Petey told him.

"What about college?" Gram asked. "You can't spend all that money on a boat."

"I'm going to."

"No sir, Petey," Granddad said. "Deven saw you coming a mile off. The way he's used that boat, she'll be no good to you. Leaks all the time, doesn't she?"

"Yes sir."

"Sure. He's left her chafing on the end of that wharf of his more times than you can count. He's just never taken proper care of her."

"I can fix her up."

"Maybe. Be quite a job, though."

"I can do it."

Gram took hold of his shoulders and made him face her. "Listen to me, Petey. Don't you want a chance to make something of yourself? Do you really mean to settle for lobstering when you could go on in your schooling and become a doctor or an engineer? If you're bound to work on the water, couldn't you go to the Maritime Academy first?"

He looked up at her and saw all her hope for him there on her face and in her eyes. He could make her happy with a word and he wanted to make her happy, but he couldn't say what she wanted him to.

"Go ahead," she said at last, releasing his shoulders. He was surprised to see tears in her eyes. "Be like your father."

"I've got to buy the *Wild Wind* from Mr. Deven.

Doesn't mean I won't make something of myself. I will."

Gram turned away from him. Outside the windows the fog seemed to press in at them. The gray whiteness hid the trees, the lawn, the cove.

"How are you going to get the five hundred dollars?" Granddad asked him.

"Hauling with you, saving all I can. I'll still pay my board."

"How long do you have?"

"Until September first. But I put that twenty dollars down."

"Won't make it. Not between now and then."

"I'll get some odd jobs on days we don't haul."

"And if you don't hand over the rest of the money in time, Deven keeps your down payment?"

"Yes sir."

"I thought you were a sharper trader than that."

"Petey can work with me on the truck," Leo spoke up. "Okay, Dad? On days you don't haul, like today. I'll see to it he makes enough."

Petey was surprised. He had never been able to figure out whose side Leo was on.

Leo smiled at him. "All right with you, Petey? Or is garbaging beneath you?"

"No sir!"

"What are you going to use for a truck?" Granddad asked. Petey knew he was saying yes.

"We'll find one," Leo said. "How about another cup of coffee? To celebrate the new partnership, and the future return of *Wild Wind.*"

Gram refilled their cups without saying a word.

"We'll walk over the back way to see Red Hartwell," Leo told him when the two of them were outside. "He has that old dump truck he isn't using, now he's in the taxi business."

Petey was still struggling with the blue, hooded sweatshirt he had pulled on as they left the house. "He'll want all he can get for it."

Leo grinned. "From me that won't be much."

Before they reached the main road, they cut to their right onto a rutted track through the alders. "Fog's as thick as I've ever seen it," Leo commented.

"I hope it burns off. Mr. Deven promised to let me take out the *Wild Wind* this afternoon."

Beyond the alders the ruts turned sharply up by the house where Petey had once lived with his mother and father. All the windows were boarded over with rough planks, which had shrunk as they aged, leaving wide gaps. The front door was nailed shut, and the gardens his mother had tended were overgrown now, the flowers choked off and gone.

They hurried on across a back field, then through a line of cedar trees where the ruts disappeared and the track became a narrow path. At a tiny cemetery Petey stopped by his father's grave. It was the only one there that showed signs of being looked after.

"You take good care of it," Leo said. He sat on the curbing and lit a cigarette.

"Gram does the most. She planted the flowers."

Leo wiped the moisture off his forehead with one sleeve of his shirt. "Miss your mother?"

"A little."

"She'll come back someday."

Petey kicked at a stone. "I don't believe she will."

"Why? She was here for a long visit last summer."

"She has that new husband now."

"So what? She still cares about you."

"Maybe."

"She just doesn't like living here. Never did."

"That's the truth."

"You pretend you're so tough, Petey. Fact is, you're soft as a pumpkin inside."

Petey struck out along the path.

"Wait up!" Leo yelled. Petey began to run, but Leo quickly caught up with him. He was laughing. "What's your hurry?"

"I just can't wait to see Red Hartwell cheat you on that old truck of his."

"Oh ho, Petey. We're partners now, remember?"

Petey slowed down.

"I'm sorry I called you a pumpkin. Honest I am, Petey."

Petey saw his teasing smile, but he couldn't stay mad at Leo for long. "I don't care if my mother comes this summer or not," he said.

Leo shook his head. "When we get to Hartwell's place, let's appear like we don't really need his truck."

Red Hartwell lived on the North Quarry Road. When the path disappeared altogether, Petey and Leo had to walk through the fog-drenched grass at the edge of a swamp. By the time they reached the hill above Hartwell's farmhouse, they were soaked.

Hartwell was sitting on a tree stump in his front yard

with his arms on his knees, his hands knotting a piece of grass. His belt was open to give his stomach room to expand, and his neck was completely hidden by the rolls of fat that disappeared inside the collar of his plaid shirt.

"Something you want, Leo?" he demanded hoarsely as they walked to him.

While Leo was haggling with Hartwell over whether or not he was going to buy Red's truck, a door slammed and Wilbur Hartwell, Red's son, walked out and joined them in the back yard. The skinny, brown-faced boy stopped close by to stare at them sullenly.

"I'm not even sure I want a dump truck," Leo was saying. "Be kind of unhandy around people's driveways."

"What's wrong with your pickup?" Hartwell asked.

"Nothing much. Needs a little work here and there before I can get a sticker."

"My truck's got a sticker, good for four more months."

Petey studied the object of their bargaining doubtfully. The ancient Chevrolet was at least six separate colors where as many layers of paint showed through. The cab door on the passenger side was tied shut with a frayed piece of rope, and the body itself was piled high with rocks, roots and rusty tin cans.

Wilbur slouched closer to Petey. "What's so damn funny, boy? You want your nose popped?"

Petey met his look. "Some truck. Bet she doesn't even run."

"She runs good," Red insisted. He walked around to the driver's side and climbed in, ground the starter a long while before the engine coughed and roared into life. He backed the truck to the corner of his house, then drove ahead to where they stood, switched off the engine and sat looking down at them.

"Make me an offer."

"Dump body work?" Leo asked.

Hartwell nodded.

"Let's see it."

"Not unless you want to load all that junk back on her yourself," Hartwell said. "Take my word for it."

Leo winked at Petey. "That's what I'm afraid of."

"They sure got a lot of mouth," Wilbur said loudly. "Want me to run 'em off?"

Hartwell shook his head. "Give them a chance, Wilbur. I think they want to do business here by and by."

The arguing over price began. Leo offered twenty-five dollars; Hartwell demanded a hundred. Petey walked slowly around the truck, shaking his head. Wilbur followed him.

"I'm going to flatten you," he hissed, "you say one more damn thing about this truck I don't like."

Petey continued his inspection. By the time he had come full circle, Hartwell was down to sixty dollars and Leo was up to forty.

"Well, Red, what do you say?" Leo asked.

Hartwell sat down in a wheelbarrow and looked at his hands. "Fifty-five."

"Let's go, Petey," Leo said. "We'll get a truck somewhere else."

They walked around to the front of the house. A heavy, gray-haired woman was hanging clothes on a line strung between two gnarled apple trees. She glanced at them a moment, then wheeled around to slap one of the children pulling on her skirt.

"Hold up," Hartwell called.

The sale was completed quickly now at fifty dollars. Hartwell told Wilbur to go inside and write up a bill of sale. When he came out with the paper, Leo handed over the money to Red.

"Fifty dollars," Hartwell mumbled. "You sure know how to take advantage of a guy." He folded up the bills and pushed them into his pocket.

Leo shook his head. "Don't take it so hard, Red. You can't win them all."

Hartwell brought the truck from the back and left it for them next to his taxi. As Leo got in behind the wheel, Petey untied the rope on the other door and climbed in beside him, holding the door shut with his arm.

"I hope she blows up in your stupid faces," Wilbur yelled.

Leo waved and started the engine. When they reached the road, he turned toward town.

"Who got took, you or Hartwell?" Petey asked.

Leo laughed. "Well, I'll give you good odds the dump body doesn't work. I let Hartwell think he fooled me on that. We'll grab my shovel from the pickup when we go by."

They roared along through the fog. "Hartwell acted pretty discouraged about the price," Petey said.

"I'll tell you, Petey, we didn't either of us get away with much." He stuck a cigarette between his lips and fished out his lighter. "And that, my boy, is life."

SIX

Garbaging

At the town dump they found out Leo was right. When they tried to raise the dump body there was only a high-pitched whine. Leo nodded slowly and shut off the engine. Using the shovel Petey had retrieved from the pickup on the way down, they took turns pushing off the trash.

"I'll go over to Grant Harbor tomorrow to change the registration," Leo said as he watched Petey roll a large boulder toward the edge of the tailgate. "I guess we can use her today without anyone being the wiser."

The boulder dropped to the ground, then tumbled over the edge of the cliff and slammed onto the top of an abandoned car twenty feet below. "Your turn," Petey said.

Leo was studying the sideboards. "Keep thrashing a while. I have to figure just how I want to build up these sides. Maybe we can use the plywood from the pickup."

After Petey finished cleaning out the body, they drove to town. As they neared the harbor, the fog grew even thicker.

"Where are we going to start?" Petey asked.

44

"I finished all but Shallow Harbor yesterday."

"Why don't we try to find some new customers? We can do Shallow Harbor this afternoon."

Leo nodded, but his face was doubtful. "We can try. Truth is, new customers are hard to get."

"With me helping you, we could double the size of your route."

"If you say so. We'll go up on Herring Street. I don't collect from a single house there."

Leo turned onto a narrow street and stopped by the first two houses. While Leo crossed over, Petey went up a cracked cement walk toward an unpainted frame house, half hidden behind a screen of bushes and vines. An old man answered his knock, opening the door three inches to stare out at him suspiciously.

"Well, what is it, boy?"

Petey took a deep breath. "I'm helping my Uncle Leo get some new customers for his garbage route."

The old man's expression didn't change. "How much?"

"Leo usually gets fifty cents for all you have."

"Fifty cents! What do you want to be, boy, Rockefeller overnight? Tiny Hooper used to charge a quarter."

"Who was he?"

"That was back before the war."

"Oh. I guess times change."

"Who says so?" The old man opened his door wide and wagged a finger at Petey. "A quarter is all I'm going to give you. If it was enough for good old Tiny, it's enough for you."

Petey shrugged and followed the old man into his kitchen. The room was stiflingly hot. On the table a huge gray and white cat was busily lapping from a small pitcher of milk.

"Be gone with ya!" The old man picked the cat up by his neck and threw him behind the stove. While he counted out pennies from a dusty peanut butter jar, Petey loaded himself up with bags of rubbish from a pile in the corner next to the sink.

He had to make three trips to the truck. When he came back to be paid, the old man dropped twenty-five pennies into his outstretched hand.

"There now, boy, that's fair pay. You come back next week, hear? I'll have some more for you then."

The door shut firmly behind him. Petey trotted to the truck. "Got twenty-five cents."

Leo was smiling.

"How did you make out?"

"The lady over there spent five minutes telling me why she didn't deal with garbagemen. Said they couldn't be trusted."

"Bound to get better," Petey said, more to himself than to Leo.

They climbed into the truck and drove along the street. The house Petey tried next belonged to the high school principal, Mr. Bristol. He invited Petey in and made him sit in a chair while he asked him all about his new work.

"I think this is just great, Petey," he said. "I didn't think you had it in you."

Petey was embarrassed. "Right now we're trying to get as many new customers as we can."

"Sure, don't let me hold you up. Never stand in the way of a dynamic businessman, I always say." He guided

Petey to the door. "I'd let you haul ours, but I take it to the dump myself. Only exercise I get!"

The door slammed. Back at the truck Leo was struggling with a mattress. Petey took the other side, and together they pushed it up into the body, on top of a fresh mound of garbage.

"Did you get all that at one place?" Petey asked.

Leo nodded.

"For fifty cents?"

"Yeah. With a deal like we're offering, we just have to hope it evens out in the end."

Petey's next customer was Mrs. Coughlin, the police chief's wife. She explained at the start that she wouldn't be able to pay him, but he felt sorry for her because half her kitchen was filled with garbage, so he took it all on credit. By this time they had a good start on a load and had taken in a dollar and twenty-five cents, Leo having made another half dollar from the family across the way.

Leo wrote Mrs. Coughlin down in his notebook, and they went on. No one was home at the next house. When they stopped beside the plumber's trailer, he came out to tell them he had just gone to the dump.

"But I've got a job for you if you want it," he said.

They followed him around to the back of his property. "See that stone wall there all fallen down?" the plumber asked. "I'll pay you twenty dollars to build it up the way it was."

Leo seemed to be counting the stones. "Been down a while, hasn't it, John?"

"Yeah, I asked you five years ago if you wanted to rebuild it."

"I recollect you did."

"With the boy here helping you, it shouldn't take long."

"Be a job. We'd have to dig some of those larger stones right out of the ground."

"We can do it," Petey said.

"And we'd have to find a way around that tree that's grown up there."

"I don't want anything fancy," the plumber said. "Just a stone wall more or less the way it was before."

Leo nodded. "We'll try to get down here to do it soon as we can. Fair enough?"

"Sure." The plumber winked at Petey. "You see to it your uncle keeps his word."

"I will," Petey told him. The moment he spoke, he knew he shouldn't have. By the time they got back to the truck, Leo was swearing in a low, steady whisper.

"Going to watch over me, Petey?" Leo asked, imitating the plumber's flat-toned voice.

Petey shook his head. He knew he had crossed the forbidden line. With Leo he was never sure where it was.

"Going to see to it I tend to my work?" Leo demanded.

"No sir. I didn't mean it that way."

"I let you in as partner, but this is my business and I do as I want and nobody tells me what to do."

They drove to the end of the street where together they carried out a large collection of broken furniture and old clothes from a garage behind Aunty Noonan's house. When they were done, Aunty and her sister had disappeared. Petey knocked on the side door and then on the front, but no one answered.

Leo called to him from the truck. "Probably turned off their hearing aids. Come on, you'll never raise them now."

Petey walked slowly back to the truck, piled high with the trash they had collected. From the cab Leo grinned down at him fiercely.

"Business is booming," he said.

Petey looked toward the waterfront to hide his disappointment. He could barely make out the dim shapes of two lobster boats at their moorings. The rest of the harbor was smothered within the wet, pressing fog.

"We might as well go have an early lunch," Leo said.

Petey turned and studied the last house left. "Try one more?"

"What's the use?" Leo asked. "Poet Jones lives there. He just got back from the hospital."

"Maybe he has something. We can at least finish the street."

"Go ahead, if you're so set on it. I'll wait here."

Petey walked to the house along an overgrown path. He climbed the granite steps leading to a side door and rapped on the curtain-shrouded glass. As he waited, a gust of fog wind blew up from the harbor into the street.

The wind was cold. After a long wait the door opened, and a tall, thin man smiled down at Petey with a puzzled look in his pale eyes. Below his wispy, white hair, the skin of his face was pulled tightly over protruding cheekbones. His smile seemed fixed, until Petey realized he wasn't smiling at all but was simply looking down at him.

Petey explained why he was there. Poet Jones bobbed his head several times and backed into the shadows behind the door.

"Come in," he said. "I'll see what I have. Come in."

Petey had to wait in a cluttered front room by a table burdened with books, papers, and dirty dishes while Poet Jones scratched around in a darkened corner. Thinking he heard a voice softly whispering, Petey looked around for someone else, but there was no one. He realized Poet Jones was talking to himself.

Petey shivered. The room was cold and damp and smelled like a cave.

"I've been away," Poet Jones mumbled. He knocked over a line of bottles, filling the room with a clatter of glass. "Been in the hospital. Bad heart. Haven't had time to get organized. There!"

He crawled out of the corner with a large box overflowing with empty beer cans and TV dinner cartons. As he set it down on the table, he tipped over a pile of books. His thin hand stabbed out and caught one. The rest tumbled to the floor. Holding the book up to the dim light that came from the curtained front windows, he peered at it intently, then leafed through the pages.

"Good, oh good, this is the one I've been looking for." His fingers made light rubbing sounds on the paper as he flipped back and forth through the book. Then he stopped and held the book higher to catch more light and began to read in a quick, firm voice:

> "Loneliness is like an iron cloud
> That sinking to the bottom of the sea
> Awaits discovery.
> In the silt of time
> Below the waves
> It rests;
> And found by explorers eons hence

Is mistaken for the refuse of
Ancient tribes of nautical Indians,
Who roamed the oceans of the world
Before becoming lost."

Poet Jones stopped and tossed the book back onto the table. "I wrote that a long time ago. Who are you?"

"Peter Shannon."

"Take this box. It's all I can find now. I've got to clean up this house. I'm going to sell, move away. Can't stand any more Hunter Island winters."

He reached into his pocket and brought out a grimy, tattered dollar bill. "Here, keep it. It's all I have."

Peter felt the twenty-five pennies in his pocket. "I'll get some change."

"No. Most people are afraid of me here on the island. They think I'm strange. I had a wife, but she left me. I just got out of the hospital. She sent me a get-well card. It was all painted with roses. I hate roses. She knows I hate roses."

Petey picked up the box and turned around, looking for the door. "Thank you," he whispered.

Poet Jones followed him outside and stood shivering in the fog. "Are you afraid of me?"

Petey stopped to look back at him from the middle of the path. "A little," he called.

Poet Jones stared at him while the foggy wind fluttered his thin shirt.

Petey wanted to say he was sorry, but the words wouldn't come into his dry throat. Finally he had to run for the truck. After tossing up the box, he jumped into the cab where Leo was smoking a cigarette.

"Took you long enough."

"I got a whole dollar," Petey said.

When they passed the house on their way back along the street, Poet Jones was gone and his door was closed.

Leo was over the worst of his anger. Instead of stopping for lunch, he drove onto the next side street where they collected rubbish for another hour. By the time they pulled into Swift's garage to buy gas and oil, they had made over six dollars and there wasn't room on the truck for another bag.

"That's a lot of new customers," Petey said.

Leo nodded.

The fog was becoming much brighter overhead as they headed for the parking lot. "Burn off in another hour," Leo said. "Let's get a couple of those big sandwiches over at Ellie's and eat in the poolroom."

In the tiny grocery store beside the parking lot Leo bought two Italian sandwiches and a six-pack of beer. When they crossed the street to the Half Tide Pool Room, Petey saw the Tates' pickup truck parked in front. Remembering his ride with them last night, he was reluctant to go inside. But there was no way he could avoid them.

The poolroom was crowded with men on their lunch break—lobstermen kept in by the fog, workmen from the boatyard, a few of the loafers who spent the greater part of every day in or around the Half Tide. Spider and Danny Tate were playing a game of points on a table near the door to the back room. Cud Baxter, the bent and wizened old man who owned the poolroom, was behind the glass counter where he sold cigarettes, pipe tobacco, playing cards, hunting knives, ammunition, and hot smoked sausages in cellophane wrappers. He nodded to Leo and Petey as they came in. "Canada's in back. Got a good game going."

Leo sat down on a bench and opened their sandwiches. When Petey returned from the Coke machine, Spider Tate looked over at him. Petey stuck out his tongue. In the crowded room no one but Spider noticed.

They ate their lunch while watching two games of eight ball on the nearest table. Leo finished his sandwich and opened one of his cans of beer. He drank it slowly, a faraway look in his eyes.

"Let's go in back a minute," he said.

"What?"

"In back." He picked up his six-pack and threaded his way through the crowd. Petey followed. As they passed the Tates' table, Spider reached out and grabbed Petey's arm.

"Did you tell your grandfather what I said about the Triangle Ground?"

"No," Petey said. "Slipped my mind. I guess it just didn't seem important to me." The voices around them were suddenly hushed.

"Let go of him," Leo said from the doorway to the back room. His voice was almost a whisper.

Spider dropped Petey's arm and began to line up a shot. Petey was about to jar his cue stick when Leo pulled him away.

"What was that all about?" he asked.

"Nothing."

In the back room Canada and three other lobstermen

were sitting at one of the card tables. Canada looked up
and grinned at them.

"Coming in for a hand, Leo? Just a little stud."

Leo took out the small cloth bag in which he was
keeping the money he and Petey had collected. Petey
saw the coldness behind the other men's smiles, and he
tried to get Leo's attention.

"We have to do Shallow Harbor," he said. "And I've got
to take out the *Wild Wind.*"

"Yeah, I know." Leo sat down in the fifth chair. "Be
right with you, Petey."

While Canada dealt the first two cards, Petey went
over to the next table and sat down. He watched the men
play a while, saw Leo win a small pot and then lose one.
The dark, windowless room was heavy with cigarette and
pipe smoke. His full stomach made him sleepy. As he
watched the cards flick around the table, the noise from
the poolroom faded into the distance. He started to doze
off, then caught himself and woke up just in time to see
Leo throw the last of their money into the pile at the
center of the table.

"I call," he said. "What do you have?"

The man across from Leo squinted through the smoke
of his cigarette. "Flush, queen high." He turned the fifth
diamond over and leaned forward for the money. "Beats
your two pair."

Leo pushed his cards away and reached for his beer.
"Ready to go, Petey?"

"Yeah."

On their way out he heard one of the men laugh. He
turned around, but the cards were flying about the table
again, and the faces of the men were cast down in
shadow.

SEVEN

"A Girl Like Sheila Wilson"

Outside the poolroom the sun was shining through the fog. The glaring light burned Petey's eyes. He noticed the Tates' pickup was gone as he and Leo crossed the street.

"I was supposed to tell Granddad the Tates mean to drive us off the Triangle Ground," he said as they climbed into their truck.

"Just mouth," Leo muttered.

"Are we going to dump this load before we head for Shallow Harbor?" Petey was trying hard to keep the disappointment out of his voice. Leo had lost the money. There was no bringing it back.

Leo nodded. On the way out of town he opened another can of beer, holding it on the seat between his legs when he wasn't drinking. The fog was scaling up rapidly now.

"That's the last time I play cards in that room," Leo said abruptly. He reached over and punched Petey's shoulder. "Hear me?"

"Yes sir." Petey couldn't stop a grin. They roared on toward the dump.

When they got back to town, Leo turned up Signal Hill and drove out on Shallow Harbor Road. They rolled through a series of long curves and over steep, wooded hills until they reached the village that encircled the smaller harbor. By then the sky was clear and the fog was a smoky white wall far out over the water.

They worked for more than two hours among the houses there, adding several new customers to the ones Leo hauled for already.

"How've we done?" Petey asked when the truck was well loaded. He was breathing hard and sweating and had long since discarded his sweatshirt. He was in a hurry to finish in time to go out in the *Wild Wind*.

Leo opened his moneybag and peered inside. "Not bad, Petey. Got to be way over ten dollars here. Another five or six dollars I wrote down in the book."

They climbed back into the truck. "Any more houses?" Petey asked.

"Just the Wilson sisters." Leo drove the truck up a dirt road away from the harbor. "Might as well get theirs."

"We haven't much room left," Petey said.

"There's enough."

"What time is it?"

"I don't know. Three-thirty or four."

"I don't want to be late getting down to Mr. Deven's wharf."

"You won't be late. What's the matter?"

"Nothing."

Leo finished a can of beer and threw it out the window in the general direction of the back of the truck. "The Wilson sisters aren't so bad. No reason to be afraid of them."

"Who's afraid?" The cab was hot and smoky. Petey pushed his head out the window for a breath of fresh air.

"No one, I guess." Leo began to laugh softly to himself.

They rounded a corner and swerved down a driveway dividing an uncut lawn. Leo backed in beside a rambling, two-story house that followed the uneven slant of the ground until it ended in a roofless shed a few feet from the edge of a cove. Three of the upstairs windows were broken, the widest gaps stuffed with blankets. The front door was nailed over with rough, gray boards. The side door leaned open on one hinge.

Petey was reluctant to go inside. He had heard stories about Sheila Wilson's sisters, about the wild parties they gave for the heavier drinking lobstermen and the drummers who came to sell on the island.

Leo led the way to the side door. He had his last can of beer jammed into his back pocket. He went inside without knocking.

"Hello, Sheila," Leo said. "Ruth and Barbie around?"

Sheila looked up from the kitchen table where she was sitting with Wilbur Hartwell. She smiled hesitantly, first at Leo, then at Petey.

Wilbur grinned at them over his cup of coffee. "The garbage boys are here. Three cheers. You want to talk to Sheila, you got to let her see your mouth moving. She's deaf as a haddock."

"Yeah, we know," Petey said.

"If you've come to see my sisters, they're on the mainland today," Sheila said. Petey watched her get up and walk to the stove. The heat in the kitchen made it hard to breathe.

Leo sat down heavily on a chair in the corner and

opened his beer. "Petey's helping me get new customers, Sheila," he said slowly. "Got anything you want hauled away?"

Sheila caught Petey staring at her. She smiled, her large brown eyes moving quickly over him. "Petey, you're a garbageman!"

Wilbur cackled loudly. Petey's face began to burn. He knew Sheila was watching his mouth, waiting, but he couldn't think of anything to say. As the sting of her taunt buried itself inside him, he was wondering why he had never before noticed that she was pretty.

"There's some garbage in the shed," she told him. "Want to take it?"

"Go to it," Leo said. "I have to rest over this beer."

Petey nodded angrily and followed Sheila out through a series of damp, empty rooms to the shed at the far end of the house. She stopped in the last doorway and pointed to a heap of paper bags.

"That's it," she said. "I'm afraid it's a little soggy."

The door to the lawn was open. Petey grabbed up an armful of bags and headed for the truck. When he came back, Sheila had disappeared.

"Half a load right here," he growled to himself. He picked up all he could carry and made another trip. He wondered if Leo had known all along what a mess it was going to be and had stayed inside on purpose.

Each time he reached the truck, he had to throw on all he was carrying, then climb up over the sideboards to stow the bags so that they wouldn't fall off. He kept forcing himself to go faster until he was soaking wet and his eyes burned with angry tears.

When he realized he couldn't get any more on, he

searched in the grass at one side of the yard until he found some boards. With these he built up one corner of the body so that he could pile on the rest of his load. Breathless and choking, he at last finished and returned to the kitchen.

Sheila was sitting on Wilbur's lap, drinking from his coffee cup. Leo hadn't moved.

"Look at him!" Wilbur shouted. "That boy really looks like a garbageman now."

Sheila squirmed away from Wilbur. "I can't pay you, Petey," she said. A smile came and went on her lips, as if she had started to laugh at him and then changed her mind. "I'm sorry. My sisters took all the money with them to the mainland."

"There you go, Petey," Leo said from the corner. "Your education is complete."

"I don't care," Petey said.

"Would you like to clean up?" Sheila asked him.

He nodded. She took him upstairs to the bathroom and stood watching him while he tried to wash.

"You don't like me, do you?"

He shrugged and went on scrubbing.

"I'm sorry I tricked you. It was just a joke."

"It was very funny."

She grabbed his arm and made him turn to face her. "I can't tell what you're saying if you don't look at me."

"I said your joke was very funny."

She started to grin, then bit her lip. What pale sunlight managed to seep through the dirty, cracked window above the sink was reflected in her dark hair. Petey found he could not continue to meet her eyes. He grabbed a towel and began drying his face.

"Wait a second, Petey. You missed a spot." She picked up the washcloth and rubbed at a place on his neck. "There, that's better."

He was becoming used to the distortion in her voice. Now that he could understand everything she said, he discovered that the difference in the sounds of her words was strangely pleasant, strangely attractive, like an accent from another country.

Still holding the washcloth she let her hand rest lightly on his shoulder. "Have you ever kissed a girl, Petey?" Before he could answer, she leaned forward and kissed his lips. "There. Now you have."

•

On the way to the stairs Petey noticed the same broken windows filled with wadded-up blankets that he had seen from the outside. The wallpaper in the hall was loose and torn and stained with moisture around the chimney.

Sheila had stopped to watch him. She looked suddenly unsure of herself. "We haven't been able to do much fixing up around here since Mom died. My sister Barbie keeps saying when it falls down around us, we'll sell out to summer people who want shore property. Then I guess we'll move to the mainland."

In the kitchen Wilbur had switched on the radio above the sink, and the moment they came in, he grabbed Sheila in his arms and began spinning her around the room in time to the music. She laughed and tried to pull away, but Wilbur wouldn't let her go.

They bumped into the table, tipping it over in a crash that sent coffee cups, ash trays and everything else tumbling into the corner. Wilbur twisted Sheila around until her back came against his chest.

"Let's have a little party," he said loudly. "I know there's rum around here some place."

Petey saw Sheila's terrified eyes. "Leave her alone."

Wilbur paid no attention to him. He put his mouth on Sheila's ear. "You can't hear me, Sheila, so I'll tell you what . . ."

Petey swung his fist into Wilbur's face. Wilbur staggered to one side and reached up to explore his lower cheek. Sheila had darted away, but stopped to watch them from behind the stove.

Wilbur flew at him, making wild noises and swinging both fists. For a moment Petey was unsure and paid for his confusion as sharp punches cut into his face and chest. He jumped back to avoid Wilbur's attack and looked toward Sheila.

"I'm going to kill you!" Wilbur screamed.

There was a flash of pain in Petey's left eye. He forgot his doubts then and hit back. They fought across the kitchen and around to the stove. Finally Petey managed to pin Wilbur's right arm behind him, using all his strength to hold Wilbur against the wall.

"Quit?" His voice was nearly lost in the noise of their breathing. "Quit?" He put more pressure on the arm. Wilbur squirmed harder but wouldn't give in.

"That's enough." Leo pushed Petey back toward the overturned table. Wilbur spun around to face them, but he didn't charge again. Instead, he ran to the outside door. They could hear his feet digging up the driveway toward the road.

"Now let's head for town," Leo said. "You've had a busy day."

"Wait a minute." Petey looked around, but Sheila was gone.

When Petey couldn't find her downstairs, he went up to the second floor, where he came upon her in a small, darkly shadowed room. She was lying motionless on a narrow cot, her face pressed against a rolled-up blanket.

"Sheila, are you okay?" he asked. Then, remembering she couldn't hear him, he went over to the cot and touched her shoulder. She slowly turned over and looked up at him.

He saw that she had been crying, and he felt more confused than ever. "Are you all right?"

When she didn't answer, he leaned closer to repeat his words. She clawed at the blanket and squirmed away from him to the end of the cot.

"Get away from me," she moaned. "Leave me alone."

Surprised and hurt, he backed away. "I'm sorry, I . . ."

"Get out! Go away from me. I don't ever want to see you again. Don't come to my house. Never, never, never!"

He walked to the door, but he couldn't resist looking back at her. "I don't like you anyway."

But she had already hidden her face in her arms so she hadn't read his lips, and his words went out into the tiny room uselessly like the pieces of afternoon that came through the holes in the window shade and lighted nothing.

EIGHT

~~~~~~

On the Triangle Ground

"How are you going to explain that eye at home?"
Leo asked him as they drove toward town.

Petey touched the tender swelling. "I don't know."
He was too tired to care. "Tell them anything you want."

Leo laughed. "Cheer up. You have a good afternoon
for your boat ride."

"Yeah, if we get there in time."

"We will."

On the way down the street Leo stopped and bought
two pint bottles of beer, then went to the tax collector's
office to fill out the papers on the truck. When they
finally pulled in by Mr. Deven's wharf, Petey was re-
lieved to see the *Wild Wind* still tied up and waiting.
The tide was high enough to float her, but there was no
sign of the undertaker.

Leo passed the time sipping his beer and watching the
schooner *Island Belle* work her way into the harbor.
Long before she had dropped anchor, Petey grew bored
with the antics of her passengers on deck. He climbed
down into the *Wild Wind.*

"Look at all those women," Leo called from above.

Petey was prying up some of the boards in the platform to check the timbers beneath. "Look at them yourself. I'm busy."

His inspection was only half begun when he heard Mr. Deven greeting Leo. Petey stood up and watched them both climb down the ladder.

"Doesn't seem to be leaking much right now," Petey said.

"That's good." Mr. Deven looked around at the torn-up platform. "Well, any time you decide to put her all back together, we can be off."

While Mr. Deven started the engine, Petey replaced the loose boards. Then he climbed up on the wharf to take the rocks Leo handed to him. After casting off the lines, he scrambled on board as Mr. Deven guided the boat out stern first into the harbor.

"She's all yours, Petey," he said, stepping away from the wheel. "Just don't pile her up on the ledges."

Petey took the wheel, slipped the gearshift into forward gear and swung the *Wild Wind*'s bow toward the mouth of the harbor. The three of them talked and joked awhile, but as they left the harbor astern and moved out into the open water beyond the inside ledges, the mood changed. Mr. Deven went to sit on the stern. Leo climbed out onto the bow with his bottle of beer and lay on his side looking down at the water. Petey, alone at the wheel, quickly forgot both of them.

The fog had rolled out to sea beyond a group of small islands south of Hunter. Petey steered toward the nearest of them, a high, rust-colored ridge that sloped down steeply at both ends like a loaf of bread. The vibrations of the engine rose up through his feet and sang inside his chest and in his throat. He and the *Wild Wind* rolled together over the low, long-backed swells. She seemed to speak to him as she carried him, seemed to whisper and remember. He held the wheel by the spokes that his father had carved and sanded smooth one by one on evenings long ago. They were still here for Petey's hands. The boat was still here, and he could remember the way it had been.

He circled the small island, rich brown in the afternoon sun. Mr. Deven came forward and began to whistle through his teeth. Leo stood up on the bow, saluted Petey and threw his empty bottle over the side. Petey finished his circle and headed for Hunter Island, where the specks of the harbor flashed below Signal Hill.

The air, all of a sudden, was cold on his skin.

"Here comes the fog," Leo shouted.

Petey looked back and saw that the island they had circled was now gone. He could see the clear outline of the fog bank, and yet the air around them already seemed part of the fog—colder, heavier, filled with a speckled dampness.

"Let me take her," Mr. Deven said.

Petey ignored him. He pulled the throttle wide open and the *Wild Wind* shot ahead. Leo joined them under the deckhouse roof. He was shivering. Before they reached the outermost ledge, he was bending over the side, violently sick.

"What's the trouble with him?" Mr. Deven asked. "It isn't that rough."

When Leo rejoined them, his face was deadly white.

"Fog's coming in fast, Petey," he shouted. "Know your way through the ledges if she shuts in?"

"I think so." Petey checked the compass several times as they roared on toward the harbor. The dangerous thing would be to get caught by the fog while still running the gauntlet of the ledges between here and the harbor. He had been fogbound with Granddad often enough, but it would be a different problem to be on his own. . . .

The *Wild Wind* charged over the swells with an exaggerated motion. Even so, Petey was surprised when Leo hurried toward the stern again. The air grew even colder as the sun faded to a feeble disk. The ledges as they passed appeared to leap at them. Yet it was as if the *Wild Wind* spoke to him, whispering assurance. When they reached the first of the channel buoys, Leo smiled weakly.

"Home free." His voice sounded stronger already.

They had beaten the fog. A few minutes later they passed the open jaws of the ferry landing.

"Take her in by my wharf," Mr. Deven told him. "I'll leave her there tonight."

When Petey climbed up to take the lines, he saw the ledges disappearing in the fog. He took a deep breath and caught the stern line Mr. Deven threw to him. If the fog had shut in on them out there, would he have been able to bring the *Wild Wind* safely home? Maybe no other boat, but he felt sure the *Wild Wind* would have given him the necessary courage, the needed skill. He felt more than ever that she was his.

On the drive home they were both silent. As Petey

stared out the window at the fog-shrouded woods, he fought against a heavy sleepiness. They parked at last in the dooryard by the house, and Leo handed him two dollars and a half.

"I know it's not much, but we'll have better days."

Petey put the money into his pocket. It was a beginning. "Did I hold up my end all right?"

Leo nodded. "You worked like a wild man." He opened his door and dropped to the ground.

Petey followed him across the dooryard. "You still want me to work with you?"

"Sure I do." Leo stopped and waited for him to catch up. "I'm going on the mainland tomorrow to register the truck. Then we tow in the pickup and we're in business."

Granddad came out of the entry and stared at them. "About given you two up for lost."

They hurried into the house. After supper Petey climbed the stairs to his room without saying a word to anyone and fell asleep before they missed him.

The fog burned off quickly the next morning, allowing Granddad and Petey to get out to haul by eight o'clock. They hauled their traps in East Bay, then worked their way up the shore past Seal Bar toward North Head. They did well in several spots close to shore, better than they had expected.

"This is good bottom for herring," Granddad said. "Stays good. The ranker it gets, the better."

The air was warm, the sun hot, the odors of herring and brim especially rich. Petey lowered the straps on his oil pants long enough to pull off his outside shirt.

"Mean eye you got there," Granddad said, snagging one of their white and black buoys with the gaff. "Leo told me this morning you hit it on the truck."

"Yes sir."

"How did you manage that?" Granddad asked. He ran the warp around the revolving winch head and threw the buoy onto the stern. He hauled hand over hand, putting the toggle bottles on the washboard and coiling the wet warp down on the platform.

Petey didn't answer Granddad's question. He pretended to be intent on watching the trap come into view below them in the green depths of the water. Granddad slipped the warp off the winch head, and together they pulled the trap up onto the washboard.

"Didn't mean to pry," Granddad said. "Trucks can throw hard punches sometimes."

"Yes sir," Petey mumbled.

Granddad unwound the bait line from the cleat to open the door of the trap, then stepped to the wheel to put the engine in gear. There were two large lobsters in the trap, both of them well over the minimum size. While Granddad took these two counters out and cleared the trap of crabs and torn pieces of kelp, Petey pulled bones of the old bait off the line and threaded the end of the line through the eye of his bait needle. He pushed on three brim, the remains of red fish after filleting, then added a bait bag bulging with herring. Granddad slapped the door shut and wound the line around the cleat in his double figure eight, double loop knot. He checked their position before dumping the trap over the side.

Petey plugged the crusher claws on the two lobsters as they went on to their next trap. This morning he had dragged himself out of bed with a black eye. He wasn't ashamed of the way he had earned it. He had held his own against Wilbur. But he didn't think Granddad would understand about Sheila.

By North Head they had run off the hard bottom. Several traps came up slimy with mud and full of crabs. They set them closer to shore, then hauled into the narrow inlet on the other side of the point. On this side the sheer face of North Head fell away straight to the water in one sixty-foot drop. Deep in its green shadow they hauled four traps for ten counters, one so big it was just within the measure. It had torn the parlor head with its massive crusher claw, and while Petey plugged the lobster and put it into the barrel with the others, Granddad mended the head with a piece of nylon.

"Going to shed in here early this year," Granddad said. "You wait. We'll be pulling them out of these traps by and by to beat anything you've seen."

"I hope so."

"I know so." Granddad baited the trap and pushed it back into the water.

On the long ride down the shore toward Tragedy Bluff, Petey filled more bait bags, then went to stand beside Granddad at the wheel.

"Kind of quiet, ain't you?" Granddad commented, idling down to pour a cup of coffee.

Petey nodded. He had been thinking about Sheila. He couldn't get her out of his mind. Not even the rhythm of the hauling had been able to drive the thought of her away. Petey started to speak, then stopped himself.

"What is it?" Granddad asked.

"I was just wondering if Leo made the boat this morning."

Granddad shrugged. "Don't know. Probably. Him and his mainland trips. Be better for him if he did miss the boat once in a while. He'll be in good shape, time he gets home."

Petey walked to the stern. He picked up a periwinkle and threw it at their wake. The memory of Sheila's face was like salt in his mouth.

Now they would be working down the east side of Hunter Island, along the shore where they had most of their traps. They began hauling around Tragedy Bluff. They didn't do nearly as well here as they had two mornings ago, but it was not until they reached Hundred Wreck Ledges that they realized something was wrong. The tide was on the ebb, and the rocks lay partly exposed, black and gleaming in the sunlight. Outside the Ledges, the first pair came up empty.

"These damn traps have been hauled," Granddad said. "Look at these two." He pointed to the bait lines, which were simply wrapped around the cleats. They weren't tied in Granddad's usual double figure eight, double loop or in Petey's backward eight, single loop.

"Somebody hauled them," Granddad fumed. "Must have done it yesterday afternoon when the fog lifted. It cleared off for a good four hours."

Petey baited the traps, tied the doors shut and got ready to set.

"I've got a good idea who it was, don't you?" Granddad asked.

Petey nodded. "The Tates. Spider warned me the other night they were going to start trouble."

"Why didn't you tell me?"

"I thought they were bluffing. They were drunk. They grabbed me on the way to town, all wound up because we set that gear on the Triangle Ground."

"Figures." Granddad looked at him sharply. "They hurt you?"

Petey shook his head.

"What did Spider say exactly?"

"Just that we should get our traps off the Triangle Ground, and if we didn't, now that he was back, he and Danny were going to drive us off."

Granddad shoved the engine into gear and they set the pair. The rest of the traps off the Ledges brought up nothing more than snappers and crabs, the snappers all well under the legal size. The Tates had obviously taken out all the lobsters that might even remotely go the measure.

Granddad was silent and grim as they headed on down the shore. He didn't say a word as they hauled up one empty trap after another. Nearly every one had a slack or untied bait line.

While they were near the Tates' cove, Granddad set the last trap they had hauled by bouncing it hard off the stern. Petey winced and buried his face in the bait barrel to reach the brim at bottom.

"They're out right now," Granddad said, pointing to

the punt on the Tates' mooring. "Probably still hauling our gear."

"Yes sir."

"They're drunk. They got to be, else they wouldn't have hauled every last trap down the shore. Tates haven't got that kind of courage sober."

"Yes sir."

"Get out of that bait and go up forward. There's a jar with some baking soda in one of the lockers. And fetch the water jug."

Granddad was hauling their next trap when Petey climbed back over the belt that drove the winch. He finished bringing up the trap while Granddad mixed soda and water in the cup from their thermos bottle.

"Empty?" Granddad demanded. He gulped down his drink, made a face and slatted the dregs over the side.

"Yes sir." Petey threw away the crabs and reached for the bait needle. "How's your stomach?"

Granddad belched. "About the way it always gets when I run afoul of the Tates."

"You ought to see a doctor."

"Doctor be damned. It's just heartburn."

Things didn't get any better as they worked toward the Cut. Granddad finally threw down the gaff. "They're drunk," he roared. "And unless I miss my guess, they're still hauling our traps. They mean to pick us clean. Kick off that belt."

Granddad quickly put the engine in gear and gave her all the gas she'd take. The *Jenny and Susan* surged ahead.

"Where are we going?" Petey shouted.

"Out to the Triangle Ground. If the Tates are still

hauling our gear, they have to be somewhere between here and there."

They ran hard toward Triangle Rock, with a quick glance into Bottomless Cove as they went by. Granddad's face was pale and strained, Petey's hands sweating. The Buick engine pounded beside them as the boat charged the swells rolling in from the south. Petey moved around to steer while Granddad closed the deckhouse window. As they were lifted by the swells, Petey saw Triangle Rock wedged against the sky.

The southwest wind was rising, and out on the open water it blew free of the interference of land. Spray slammed off the side of the bow and slatted in sheets against the windows. Gradually Triangle Rock increased in size, standing high on the water, barren and drab except where a small patch of grass grew between two steep outcroppings of rock.

Before they approached too close, Granddad took the wheel and changed course for the Triangle Ground, a shallow area of hard bottom to the southwest of Triangle Rock. They could already see the Tates' boat, the *Pretty Lady*, hauling on the Triangle Ground, rolling in the swells. She was brown with slime, her deckhouse paint peeled off in large, discolored patches. Her side windows were covered with rough pieces of unpainted plywood.

Granddad reached under the engine-box cover to coax more speed from the Buick. Petey thought the boat was going to shake herself apart, but they were on the Triangle Ground before the Tates could clear themselves of a warp that had snarled and wound around their winch head.

Spider pulled the warp free and threw it over the side.

Petey saw the buoy near the *Pretty Lady*'s stern—it was one of Granddad's, freshly painted white and black. There weren't any of the Tates' red buoys close by.

Granddad eased up on the throttle as he maneuvered alongside. He reversed the engine, and Petey reached out to gaff the upright on the Tates' deckhouse to pull them in close. Granddad slowed the engine to an idle and shifted into neutral just as Spider Tate lurched over to the side. Danny was sitting on a lobster crate behind Spider, pretending to eat his lunch, rubbing his boots on the greasy platform. There was a whisky bottle beside him.

"Something you want, old man?" Spider demanded thickly. His long arms hung down dangerously at his sides, and his mouth was twisted into an ugly sneer.

"You're darn right," Granddad shouted at him. "I want to know what the hell you're doing out here in the middle of my gear."

"We're looking for one of our pairs we set this way, if it's any of your business."

"No, you're not!" Petey yelled from his perch on the washboard. He was holding the two boats apart so that they wouldn't roll against each other. "You've been hauling our gear ever since yesterday afternoon."

"Better watch your mouth, short stuff, 'less you want it slapped good."

Granddad's eyes bulged, his face and neck flushed a deep red. He reached out quickly and grabbed Spider's shirt front, pulling him over the side until Spider's face was only inches from his own.

"You tell Danny to hand over those lobsters."

Petey could see that Spider was frightened. He tried to

break away, but Granddad's hands were locked onto his shirt, twisting it against his throat.

Petey thought Spider would give in, but then Danny stood up and grabbed their gaff. "Can I hit him, Spider?" he asked in his whine. "Can I hit him now? Please can I hit him?"

"Go to it," Spider croaked as loudly as he could with Granddad choking him.

His hair falling in ragged strands over his eyes, Danny raised the gaff and swung it down at Granddad with deadly force. Granddad tried to duck to one side and hold onto Spider at the same time. Danny's gaff hit him a glancing blow on his forehead, and Granddad went over in a slump.

"I'll get you," Petey shouted. Everything was turning red. He snatched his bait needle and threw it at Danny. He threw the water bucket at Spider. He was so blind with fear and rage that he couldn't tell if he was hitting them or not. He threw the extra gas can, their dinner pail, the lobster measure, the nearly empty bushel of herring.

He was going forward to look for more things to throw when Danny screeched. Petey saw the gaff whipping toward him. He jumped to one side, lost his footing on the wet platform and went over on his back. By the time he got up, Spider had his boat under way and was turning off toward home.

"Get your traps off the Triangle Ground!" Spider shouted. "Or we'll cut off every damn one of them."

~~~~~~~~~~~~~~~~~~~~~~~~~~~~~~~~~~~~~~

NINE

"We Don't Want to Start a War"

Petey tried to help Granddad up, but the old man pushed him away.

"I'm all right." He crawled to the stern and sat there wiping at the bleeding gash in his forehead with his handkerchief. "Just a cut, that's all."

The *Pretty Lady* was already small in the distance, on her way back to Hunter Island. Petey looked at Granddad. Rage welled up inside him.

"If Danny hadn't knocked you out, we would have had them," he said. He knew suddenly that he was going to be sick. There was just enough time to lean across the washboard. . . .

"You all right, Petey?" Granddad quickly had one arm around him. "Are you hurt?"

Petey shook his head. He washed his face in the cold salt water. When he straightened up, Granddad kept him from moving away.

"What is it, boy? Were you frightened?"

"No."

"You're pale as can be."

"I want Spider to die the way Dad did." He was shak-

76

ing all over, and no matter how hard he tried, he couldn't stop.

"Don't talk like that, Petey." Granddad was staring at him, his own eyes wide and burning.

"I can't forget. Ever since Spider's come back from prison, I've been thinking about the way he killed Dad."

"It was a fight."

"After Dad tripped, Spider kicked him. You know it same as I do. Once he had Dad down, he kicked him to death, because he was too scared to let Dad get up again."

"We weren't there." Granddad's voice was low.

"It was right in town! People saw it. They saw Spider start the fight. Don't you care any more?"

"Listen Petey. Hal was your father, but don't forget he was my son." Granddad's hands squeezed down hard on Petey's shoulders. "Spider's been punished. We both knew he'd come back someday. Why else would Danny have stayed on all this time alone, half starving to death? Now let's have no more talk like this."

Petey finally nodded, and Granddad let him go.

"We might as well haul our traps here and head for home," he said gently. He tied his handkerchief around his forehead. "No sense going down around to sell today."

"Let's haul the Tates' traps," Petey said. "We can get back at them."

Granddad shook his head, winced and put his hand up to his wound. "No. I think they'll leave us alone now. We don't want to start a war."

Neither of them said anything more as they hauled

their traps on the Triangle Ground. Petey felt lost and confused. He wanted to strike back at the Tates, and he couldn't understand why Granddad wouldn't. He didn't think Granddad was a coward, yet where was his anger now? It was as if the fight had frightened it away. They were letting the Tates get away with far too much.

On the way in Granddad slapped Petey on the shoulder. "One thing you got to remember," he said, slowing the engine down so that he could talk without shouting. "This quarrel with the Tates goes back before you were born. Old Parker Tate and me . . . He used to give me fits. I can remember hauling out there on the Triangle Ground when your father was younger than you are now and finding half our traps gone, cut clean off."

"What did you do?"

Granddad blew out a cloud of smoke and stared into the bowl of his corncob. The *Jenny and Susan* was riding nicely in the chop. "I used to match him trap for trap. Some years we would clean each other out long before shedding time."

"But you taught him a lesson."

Granddad grunted. "You can't teach a Tate anything. All we did by warring was keep each other poor. I wish I had the price of every trap I lost to Parker Tate. I'd be a rich man now."

There was so much real regret in Granddad's voice that Petey was silenced.

"And then Parker drowned," Granddad said after a long pause.

"Yeah, I know."

"Well, think what that had to do to Spider and Danny. They were no more than boys your age then. And their father drowning on the Triangle Ground, that made it all the worse."

For a moment Petey saw Spider Tate his own age, felt Spider's loss as he felt his own. "And that's why they hate us now?"

"Hate's got a strange memory. After a while it doesn't need reasons any more."

They were back at Fox Cove by the middle of the afternoon. Granddad put their lobsters into a crate and tied it off the stern. After scrubbing down the stern deck and platform, Petey rowed Granddad to shore. Since he had thrown their dinner pail at the Tates, they had had nothing to eat on the way in. Granddad had taken two more drinks of baking soda, but Petey could tell his stomach was still bothering him.

"I promised your Gram a ride this afternoon but guess I'll lie down after lunch," Granddad told him.

"How about your head?"

"I'll be all right."

Gram Jenny served them a cold lunch of turkey sandwiches and milk with canned pears for dessert. While Granddad took his nap, Petey sat out on the porch reading old copies of the *Saturday Evening Post.* Gram came out and questioned him about their fight with the Tates.

"He won't go see the doctor," Gram said. "Stubborn! There's no man more set in his ways on all of Hunter Island."

Petey gazed out over the cove. Far off above the water the air was growing thick with haze. "The fog's coming in again."

"You like to read, don't you, Petey?"

Surprised, Petey turned to look at her. "Yeah, I do."

"And you get good grades in school." Gram's face went soft with a smile. "All your teachers say you have a quick mind."

Petey expected her to begin on college again, but she didn't. Instead, she talked about books she had read when she was young. Petey listened with half his mind, the rest of his attention focused on the deepening haze outside the bay.

"You're like your father," Gram said. "There, but not there. I'm talking to you and you're nodding your head, but we're miles apart."

The wind had shifted. It blew now uncertainly in the spruce trees around the cove. The afternoon was unusually still, as if the fog was forcing a wave of silence before it.

Gram went to the railing and inspected her flower boxes. "They look a little starved, don't they?" she said.

"I guess so."

"Foggy summers! This is going to be a bad one."

"How can you tell?"

Gram faced him. "I've lived long enough to know what to expect."

TEN

~~~~~~

The Trouble with Leo

When Granddad woke up from his nap, he and Gram headed for town in Granddad's car to do the shopping. Petey went along for the ride. The fog was in thick now, blurring the outlines of the spruce trees, turning the occasional maples into rainmakers. Granddad drove slowly, but when Leo's truck suddenly appeared out of the gray on the wrong side of the road, there was barely time for them to swerve onto the shoulder. In the soft sand, Granddad lost control of the car. A fortunate slide sent them back onto the hard dirt as Leo skidded by, all six wheels locked and dragging.

Petey looked back and saw Leo stagger out of his truck. Granddad started the stalled car and spun his tires as they left Leo standing there in the fog. Granddad's pipe had gone out, and he rammed it into the ash tray so hard the stem snapped.

"Drunk as a skunk! Could have killed us all. I'm done with that boy, I swear I'm all done."

"Will." Gram's voice sounded small against Granddad's anger.

"Well, what's the use, Jenny? He's hopeless the way

things are now. I'm sick of looking out for him, making excuses for every fool thing he does. Maybe if we booted him out on his own, he'd make some kind of effort to . . ." Granddad took a deep breath and left what he was saying unfinished.

Gram was crying. "I'd give anything to have him settle down with a nice girl."

Gram and Granddad were still talking about Leo when they reached town. "He just likes to celebrate whenever he goes on the mainland," Petey said, trying to defend him.

Granddad shut him up with a look.

There was no more said while they bought groceries in the A&P, but Petey was bracing himself for the worst on the drive back to Fox Cove. He didn't like the grim steadiness in Granddad's anger, as if he had made up his mind to something and was going to see it through no matter what.

Leo came down from his room as they carried the groceries into the kitchen from the car. He had his new sports coat on over his best trousers, but the wear and tear of his trip to the mainland showed plainly enough. His eyes were half shut, his face flushed, his shoes covered with dust.

"Are you all right?" he asked them. He was staring at the cut on Granddad's forehead.

Granddad placed the last bag on the kitchen table. "We're alive, if that's what you want to know."

Leo shook his head impatiently. "Did I give you that cut?"

"No." Granddad took a pipe from the ashtray on the stove. Leo turned to Gram.

"Look Mom, I'm sorry as I can be. I never realized I was so far over on the other side of the road and . . ."

"Petey, go out to the shed and see if you can find your father's old suitcase." Granddad looked at Gram as if to silence any objection from her.

"What's this, Mom?" Leo demanded. "What's he doing?"

"We're asking you to move out," Granddad told him. "Go on, Petey!"

Petey went outside and crossed the lawn to the shed beside Granddad's shop. He found the suitcase behind a barrel of ashes. He stood there for a moment, for he didn't want to go back in.

Granddad shouted at him from the porch. Petey picked up the suitcase and carried it inside the house. Leo was arguing with Gram. Granddad pulled the suitcase away from Petey and put it down on a chair. He took a key from a hook near the entry.

"This fits the padlock on the side door of Hal's house. You can stay there until you find something better."

Leo pushed his hand away. "I don't want it. I can't stay there. It's practically falling down."

Granddad dropped the key into Leo's coat pocket. "Won't be anyone there to care what shape you're in when you come home. Should suit you fine."

"Dad, cut it out. Go ahead and be mad. I don't blame you. I'm a fool when I drive after I've been drinking, and I'm not the son you want. I know that. I can't take Hal's place. Never could, never will. But I don't want to leave this way. I'm sorry I ran you off the road. Can't a man make a mistake? I'll straighten out, I promise."

Granddad shook his head. "You're no man." His face

flushed red. "You can't even grow up. It's not just this last thing. When I need you, you're never there. Do you think saying you're sorry makes up for all the times you've let me down? You could have killed or crippled us today, could have hurt yourself. Haven't we had enough grief? Do you have to bring more down on us with your craziness?"

"Will!" Gram cried. "Don't."

"I'll say what's on my mind," Granddad bellowed at her.

"Stop it, Dad," Leo said. "That's enough."

"Take this thing." Granddad threw the suitcase into Leo's arms. "Go pack your clothes."

Leo walked slowly to the stairs. On the first step he turned to look at them, his face twisted with emotion. "I never could be the match of you, Dad. But I've tried. I have tried so hard."

"Leo!" Gram called, but he was already pounding up the stairs.

"It's the only thing we can do," she told Petey.

The fog was in to stay. It didn't burn off the next day. It did not retreat beyond the mouth of East Bay during the week that followed. Granddad replaced all the equipment Petey had thrown at the Tates, and when they could, they hauled their traps in the bay and along Seal Bar and took the lobsters to town in the back of Granddad's car. Although they did well out of what traps they could tend, the hauls were too small for Petey's share to amount to much.

The only consolation was that as far as they knew, the Tates weren't hauling either. But as the days went by and Petey's savings grew only a little at a time, knowing everyone else was having the same luck didn't help. Everyone else didn't have the deadline to meet that he had, and September first was one day closer every morning.

Petey worked hard with Leo. They towed in the pickup, and after stripping it of everything valuable, they dumped it into the hollow with the other wrecks. They went the rounds on their garbage route, adding more customers. In between they found a few small trucking jobs. Leo never spoke of the fight that had banished him to Petey's old house. And Petey was careful never to refer to it in any way.

The Fourth of July dawned cloudy and raw. Granddad called Petey from the hall, telling him to dress warmly.

"We're hauling today, fog, wind or rain," he said.

Petey had planned to go down street to watch the parade, but he knew better than to argue with Granddad now. The fog had begun to wear on the old man's patience, and each morning his bad temper was sharper, more ready to lash out.

While they ate breakfast, Granddad tried to get a weather forecast on the living room radio, but there was too much static. He finally gave up in disgust, and they pulled on their boots and left the house to walk down to the cove. The fog, patchy and thin, blew before the southeast wind like smoke. Petey could tell the weather wasn't going to get any better. Granddad seemed to read his mind as they climbed aboard the *Jenny and Susan.*

"Rain by eleven," he growled. "See if I'm not right."

They hauled in the bay and along Seal Bar. Bait was a problem. The remnants of the brim in the barrels were so rotten Petey had to put on gloves and press the bony pieces into bait bags. He tried to be careful, but Granddad was hauling hard and fast. To keep up, Petey had to hurry himself, and the sharp, foul bones kept sticking into his hands.

There was a crate of fresher brim they had brought up from town in the trunk of Granddad's car. The car still smelled of it. They rationed this as they hauled, filling in with crabs. Petey had the job of preparing these in addition to everything else.

They finished hauling off the bar, and Granddad turned the *Jenny and Susan* toward Tragedy Bluff. They were the only boat out. Through the swirling fog they occasionally saw the rocky sides of the bluff before them.

"You're going to have to move a little better," Granddad told him as they began hauling again. "We're going through this gear just as fast as we can."

Petey helped him pull the first trap onto the washboard. He opened the door and pulled the crabs out, slinging them into a basket. The ones he had prepared were already on the bait needle with the brim. There were two counters to plug, the bait needle to fill again, then another trap to pull up from the water. And more bait bags needed filling when he had the chance. . . .

Granddad drove the engine wide open between traps.

The boat pitched and rolled, the spray drenched the platform, and the day became for Petey a race of motion against time. He moved from barrel to basket to crate to trap as fast as he could while the gray water and the gray sky revolved about him. There was no time to talk, no time to look, no time to think. He moved the way he had learned to move. There was no praise from Granddad, but the reward was there and it was fine, for Granddad did not once have to wait for him, did not once have to growl or complain. There was the work, and it went on and on like a song without an ending.

Around noon it began to rain. The wind blew harder, tearing the fog apart so that they could see the shore, then drawing the gray curtain close around them again. Petey had no cap. Rain ran down his neck inside his clothes. When he started to shiver, Granddad pressed a thermos cup of hot coffee into his hand and idled down the shore to their next trap. Petey stood under the roof next to the engine to soak up all the heat he could.

After hauling for another hour, they ate their lunch in the shelter of the Cut. Petey was starved. Granddad gave him half of his second sandwich.

"Guess the Tates are staying in today," he said. He struck a match for his corncob. "No sign of life when we passed their cove. I don't like to be the only one out. Something goes wrong and there you are."

"The Tates wouldn't help us if we were broke down, anyway." Petey finished the coffee and unwrapped the last piece of pie.

"That's true enough. Wonder where they are, though. No one's seen much of them during all this fog."

"Probably on a bat."

Granddad smiled. "That's some talk for a boy your age."

Petey shrugged. The rain slashed hard against the deckhouse roof. He was reluctant to go back to hauling. But there was nothing left to eat.

Below the Cut was the gear they hadn't hauled the day of the fight on the Triangle Ground. Most of these traps came up empty. By now the rain was a downpour that hissed angrily on the water around the boat.

They had broken several toggles while hauling, and when Granddad tied on the last of the spare bottles they kept under the stern, he shook his head. "That's enough. I'd sure like to get out to the Triangle Ground, but no sense taking a chance where we're the only ones out." He flipped off the belt with the gaff.

While Granddad steered for home through the fog and rain, Petey cleaned up the boat as much as he could. They had the two lobster barrels covered with oilcloth to keep out the rain. It had been a good haul, and Petey could almost forget about being soaked when he thought of his share.

"How much have you got saved now?" Granddad asked when Petey come forward to the wheel.

"About forty-five dollars."

"Well, with the price up another nickel I'd say you'll have over sixty by the time we get back from town."

"Hope so."

"Still leaves you a long way to go."

"I know."

When they reached the mooring, they used the outboard motor to bring the barrels one at a time to shore in the punt. Petey went after the wheelbarrow, and together they pushed, pulled and carried the barrels through the mud to the dooryard.

"If I didn't have a desk full of bills, I'd never go through all this," Granddad said when they paused to catch their breath. "And then we have to bring that stinking bait back the same way."

Rain was still pouring down when they pulled out the seat and loaded the barrels into the back of Granddad's car. Granddad carried the seat onto the porch and left it beside the door. Petey saw Gram come to one of the windows in the front room to look out at them.

"Why don't we see if Leo's home?" he asked. "Be easier to use the truck, especially for the bait."

Granddad shook his head.

They drove to town in their boots and oilskins. It was raining too hard to bother changing into anything dry. Granddad fussed with the windshield wipers the whole way.

"There's Leo," Petey said as they neared town.

Granddad slowed down and so did Leo, but only Petey waved. On Main Street the rain had turned the red, white and blue decorations for the Fourth to a pasty mess. The big orange tent in the parking lot flapped wetly in the wind.

"Guess they won't be having the fireworks tonight," Petey said. He was cold and tired, and his hands ached where all the brim bones had jabbed him. He tried to cheer himself up by thinking about the money he would be getting, but a sadness had crept inside him on the ride down that wouldn't go away.

Carl Julian was in his office when they drove up. They carried their two barrels inside where Julian had another set of scales. The two men joked with each other, but Petey hardly listened. Their laughter seemed unreal, like noises in a dream. He waited in the doorway at the edge of the rain.

After what had happened between Leo and Grand-dad, the last thing Petey wanted to do was quarrel with Leo himself. But the next day when he and Leo took the truck to town to begin picking up garbage again, there was trouble over the work.

The morning was cloudy, with the threat of more rain. Fog lay just outside the harbor, as thick and uninviting as cold pea soup. They collected on the first two streets, making only five dollars and filling half the truck. Petey could tell Leo was getting restless.

"No reason to thrash," he said for the third time. "Let's go get a six-pack and I'll treat you to a Coke."

From then on they got less and less done, and when Leo headed for the Half Tide Pool Room well before noon, there was nothing Petey could do to stop him. Leo walked into the back room where a game of poker was in progress. Petey shot several games of eight ball with Cud Baxter while he was waiting. Finally he went into the back room and asked Leo for his share of the money they had earned.

"What's the matter, kid?" Leo demanded. "Afraid I'll lose it all?"

"We're not going to collect any more garbage today, are we?" Petey asked, trying to keep the impatience out of his voice. He could feel a dangerous tension building up between them.

Leo pushed twelve quarters from his pile of change without glancing away from his cards. "Take it. The way I'm winning I don't need it. And maybe I don't need you any more, either."

"We don't have to fight," Petey said in a low voice.

"My little nephew," Leo said to the men around the table. "The saint of Hunter Island."

The men laughed. Petey took his money and walked out through the poolroom to the street.

ELEVEN

~~~~~~

Taking Sheila Home

During the gray noon hour the town was nearly empty. Petey went to stand by himself on the steps in front of the post office where he tried to figure out what he should do now that he had angered Leo. Demanding his share while Leo was playing cards had proved a poor way to get Leo back to work. Now he stood to lose a lot more than one afternoon of garbage collecting.

"There's a letter for you."

Petey looked behind him and saw Ralph Medwick, the postmaster, standing in the doorway.

"From your mother. Her new husband's name is Tyler, isn't it? Thought you might like to take it now instead of waiting until Lars brings it up in the morning."

Petey followed him inside and waited by the counter while Medwick leafed through the letters and circulars in one of the pigeonholes built into the left wall.

"Here she be," he said. He pulled out the envelope and handed it to Petey. "Your mother coming here this summer?"

"I don't know," Petey said. "Thanks."

He felt the envelope as he went out. It was thin—one

page, two at the most. But she wouldn't write a long letter if she was coming soon. . . .

Putting the envelope into his shirt pocket, he walked toward the little park beyond the ferry landing. He tried not to run, but halfway along, where the sidewalk ended and he had to use the road, he couldn't hold himself back.

He ran down a path beneath a row of spruce trees. The park covered most of a point of land jutting out into the water at the entrance to the harbor, and the fog was thicker here. He found a bench off to one side and tore open the letter.

> *Dear Petey,*
>
> I was hoping you would answer my last letter but I know your Granddad keeps you real busy. Arnold thought we should have a picture of us taken to send you and we did, only it didn't come out very good. Perhaps I'll send you a copy later.
>
> How are Gram and Leo? Does he still have his garbage collecting route? You can see I have so many questions. Won't you write me when you have time?
>
> Arnold and I were hoping to get down to the island this summer, but he's so busy at the office I'm afraid our vacation will have to wait. Isn't that just like life? The file clerks and typists all get their time off but Arnold has to keep his nose to the grindstone every day.
>
> I hope you won't be too disappointed that I can't visit you. You know you can come here to stay with us whenever you want. Isn't it time we got over our bad feelings? Hunter Island doesn't suit everyone the way it does you, and Arnold can't give up his career.
>
> Now write me soon, dear, and tell me all the news.

As I sit here I can practically taste one of Gram's blueberry pies.

Love to all,
MOM

Petey read the letter twice. He was about to tear it up when he heard someone walking on the grass near his bench.

"Why are you crying?"

He looked around and saw Sheila Wilson standing about twenty feet away. She was wearing a dirty tan raincoat. Her hair, fluffed out by the fog, fell uncovered to her back, and there were dark circles beneath her eyes. The rest of her face was chalk white.

"I'm not crying," he said. He folded his mother's letter and stood up to push it all the way into his side pocket.

"Yes you are." She walked up to him and touched his cheek with her hand. "There now, what's the matter?"

"Nothing."

"Why haven't you come to see me?"

He wondered if she was teasing him again, but there was no sound of it in her voice. "You told me not to."

She smiled faintly. "Do you believe everything girls tell you?"

He shrugged.

"I don't let Wilbur come see me any more."

"That's good." Petey backed up toward the path. She followed him.

"Petey, will you take me home?"

He stared at her as her eyes filled with tears. "What's the matter?"

"Spider Tate and his horrible brother came to our

house last night and I've been out all night and I'm so cold I think I'm going to shake apart." She took out a handkerchief and blew her nose.

"You stayed down here?"

"I walked around some. I couldn't go back, not with them there and Barbie and Ruth so drunk they don't know what they're doing."

"What happened?"

She shook her head. "I had to leave, Petey, that's all. Please don't ask me any more."

"Leo won't let me take the truck, but I can walk you home."

Sheila nodded. "Maybe they're gone now. I was just afraid to go back there all alone."

She took his hand as they walked out of the park.

When they reached her house, he saw the Tates' pickup truck in the driveway. Sheila pulled him behind a clump of alders. "They'll see us."

She was close to tears again, and he tried hard to think what to do. He touched her arm to get her attention. "Isn't there any other place you can go?"

She shook her head. "If there was, I would have gone there last night. Oh Petey, what am I going to do? I can't stay out here forever."

"Is there a back way in?"

"Just an old outside staircase. It's ready to fall down."

He took her partway up the road, then cut through the undergrowth. They came out in a tangle of wild raspberries near the far end of the house.

"Ouch! Petey, they're sharp!"

"Be quiet. If we circle around here, will they see us?"

"Not if they're in the kitchen."

"Is that where they are?"

"How do I know! Petey, do something. I'm all tangled up."

He helped her out of the thorns. Once they were clear, they ran behind the house. Sheila pointed to a rickety staircase built onto the back wall. It led to a landing on the second floor below a door without a knob.

"Can we open it?"

"What?"

"Can we open that door?"

"I think so."

He went up first, pulling Sheila over the steps that looked rotten. The staircase trembled beneath them. When he reached the landing, he edged along close to the wall of the house and pushed on the door. It gave a quarter of an inch and stopped.

"Let me help," Sheila said behind him.

He shook his head. Holding onto a loose clapboard with one hand, he swung his weight against the door, then squeezed through the opening. A moment later he pulled Sheila inside.

He looked around in the gloomy light. They were at one end of the upstairs hall. Sheila carefully pushed the door shut and led him to her room. When they were safely inside with her door closed, she began to giggle.

"That's some way to come home," she said. "Like a thief." She pulled off her raincoat and draped it over a straight-backed chair. Underneath, she was wearing a brown skirt and pink blouse. She picked up a brush from the top of her bureau and began tugging at her hair.

"I guess I'll get going now," Petey told her.

She stopped to stare at him. "You can't, Petey. Not until the Tates leave. I don't want to be alone."

He couldn't say no to the look on her face. The moment she saw that he was staying, she relaxed.

"Like to brush my hair?" When he shook his head, she laughed.

"Don't make so much noise," he told her. "They'll hear you."

"No they won't. Besides, I'm safe with you. Come on, Petey, brush my hair for me."

"No." Opening the door a crack, he listened. He could hear voices downstairs.

"They don't even know we're here." Sheila walked over to him and kissed his cheek. "That's for helping me, Petey."

He kissed her lips before he realized he wanted to. His face began to burn. She was looking at him with eyes as wide open and deep as any he had ever seen. She stood there staring at him, and he knew she was waiting and he thought he would choke on the pounding in his throat.

"I . . . I'll go see if I can find out when they're leaving," he told her quickly.

He slipped out into the hall before she could stop him.

TWELVE

~~~~~~

The Tates' Plan

He went downstairs a step at a time. From the sounds he could tell they were all in the kitchen. Spider and one of Sheila's sisters were laughing. Every few seconds Danny's whining voice would cut in with a word or two, and the other sister would go into hysterics. He heard the refrigerator open and close, heard the clink of glasses. He crouched at the foot of the stairs and waited for them to quiet down.

After a while he began to understand some of what they were saying. Then Spider spoke, and he went cold all over.

"Thanks to the Shannons, we'll soon have a lot more money coming in. We'll show you girls a real party then."

"Tell 'em how we're going to do it," Danny said. "Tell 'em how."

Spider laughed. One of the sisters squealed. It took several minutes for the commotion to die down.

"I think Sheila's kind of sweet on Petey Shannon," one of the girls said. "She plagues Leo about him every time he comes over."

"Maybe we should see if we can find her, Barbie," the other girl said. Her voice was deeper than her sister's. "She was real upset when she ran out of here last night."

"Let's go find her," Danny shouted. "Come on, Barbie! Ruth is right. We'd better find her before something bad happens."

"She'll be okay," Barbie said. "We'll have another drink instead while you boys tell us how you're planning to get rich off the Shannons."

Petey longed to move closer, but he didn't dare. Drunk as they were, he couldn't let them find out he was listening. They mixed fresh drinks as Spider told them about the fight on the Triangle Ground. His voice became hoarse with anger.

"Sounds like they caught you in the act," Ruth said.

"Yeah, well, they're going to pay for that. We've been taking it easy during this foggy spell. Soon as it clears, we're going to start hauling their traps again, a few every day. And they're going to lose gear on the Triangle Ground. That way we'll get some of the nylon warp we need."

Danny giggled. "We're going to make us extra money and buy us another boat so's we can set twice as much gear next year."

"That's right," Spider said. "Next year we'll use two boats and set so much gear on the east side them Shannons won't have room to turn around. And they're going to buy us that boat with their own lobsters."

"Suppose they catch you again?" Barbie asked.

Spider snorted. "An old man and a boy? Between the two of them they ain't got guts enough to stop us. The old man don't want to square off with me."

"Then why did he chase after you last time?" Barbie asked.

"We made a mistake and pushed him too far. Left him no choice. We'll go easy this time, steal a little here and a little there, and he won't lift a finger."

"What about the boy?"

Spider laughed. "Who's afraid of him?"

Petey had heard enough. He wanted to get home and tell Granddad. But in the upstairs hall he paused by Sheila's door. After a moment's indecision, he went into her room.

She was lying on her cot with her eyes closed, hugging her pillow. He stared down at her, then took a blanket that was folded beneath her feet and covered her. She stirred but did not open her eyes. He sat down in the chair and waited for the Tates to leave.

It was late in the afternoon when he heard their voices in the yard outside. Sheila was still sleeping. He listened for the sound of the truck driving off before he stepped out into the hall. He walked quickly to the door that opened onto the outside staircase. In a few moments he was down to the ground and running toward the bushes.

The fog was cold, and he shivered when he stopped on the road to look back at the house. There was no sign that anyone had seen him leaving. The Tates were gone and the road was empty.

He got two rides and arrived home before supper.

Granddad was down in the shop building traps. He looked up as Petey came through the door, then went back to nailing laths to the three spruce bows on his rack.

"How'd you make out today?" he asked around a mouthful of nails.

Petey sat down on the chopping block. "Leo wanted to play cards."

"I see."

"Hey Granddad?"

"What?"

"When this fog clears off, what are we going to do?"

Granddad pulled the partially built trap from the rack and sawed off the lath ends with a small handsaw. "We're going to haul traps, that's what."

"I mean about the Tates."

"We've scared them off. They won't bother us any more."

"They're planning on it, Granddad."

"How do you know?"

While Petey told him everything he had overheard at Sheila's house, Granddad set his trap on the rack and began nailing in the rocks.

"Just drunken bragging," he said. "Don't pay it no mind. What they tell the Wilson sisters and what they do are two different things."

"They sound like they mean it."

"I'm not going to lose any sleep."

Petey picked up a buoy and studied the faded paint beneath the barnacles and dried slime. He was disappointed in Granddad. He had expected a little appreciation for his warning. Instead, Granddad hardly seemed to believe him.

"It's the same as the cold war, Petey," Granddad went on. "A lot of threats, but nobody's foolish enough to really start trouble. The Tates have just as much to lose in a trap war as we do."

"What's to stop them if we don't hit back?"

"Their own lack of guts."

"That's what Spider said about us."

Granddad laughed and reached for more nails. "And you let that get under your skin."

"I think you're afraid to stand up to them. You were mad the other day, but now you've been thinking about it too long." Petey's heart was thumping hard.

Granddad put down his hammer. "I'm going to forget what you just said. I'm telling myself you're only a boy. But one more word and I'm going to turn you so black and blue your own Gram won't know you."

Petey walked to the door.

"Wait a minute," Granddad shouted. "I don't know what you were doing at Sheila Wilson's house, but you stay away from there. I don't want you getting mixed up with her kind."

That night Petey lay in bed, unable to sleep. Outside his window the fog lay over the house and the yard and the cove in damp, heavy silence. White flashes of sheet lightning pulsed within the fog. Petey listened for the first low muttering of thunder.

Supper had been a grim and silent meal, with Granddad withdrawn into his anger and Gram puzzled and impatient because they wouldn't tell her what was wrong between them. And afterwards he had not dared to visit Leo at the old house, despite the need to make up, despite the need to talk to someone.

He listened for the thunder, waited for the storm as if when it came, it would drive away all the trouble and confusion that was his life now. He lay on his side and watched the window flash in and out of darkness. . . .

It was like a dream, and he was half asleep and didn't know what was happening. There was thunder and brilliant lightning and wind in the trees beyond his window.

"Hey Petey! Wake up."

He sat up and rubbed his eyes. Between the cracks of thunder he could hear Leo singing drunkenly below his window. Petey crossed the room and took out his screen.

"Petey?"

"Yeah."

"Had to talk to you."

"You'll wake them up." A flash of lightning showed Leo standing down there, his open shirt billowing in the wind. "What is it?"

"Lost all my money again."

Petey didn't know what to say. Leo had started singing again. Thunder rumbled down the sky, drowning out the words.

"I'm sorry you lost your money."

"Hell with it. Let's go for a run."

Petey pulled on his clothes and sneakers and

climbed out the window onto the roof of the back entry. From there it was an easy jump to the ground. He landed as the whole night exploded.

"Good boy, Petey," Leo said. "Let's take off."

It started to rain as they circled the house to the road. Leo went ahead of him, shouting as the lightning snapped and the thunder broke. Petey ran madly to keep up. Everything was all right between them now. They had run like this before, and everything was fine.

THIRTEEN

Petey Strikes Back

After the rain and thunder came a rush of cool, dry northern air. The winds from the northwest carried away the fog that had smothered Hunter Island for so long. The sky cleared, the blue came back, and the sea sparkled again beneath a warm sun.

Through most of July the weather was good. In the mornings the air lay still, soaking up heat until the southwest wind began to blow. Out to haul, spray from the chop hit Petey's warm skin like a shower of cold needles. The *Jenny and Susan* rolled in her awkward but reasonable way as they hauled down through the long afternoons.

But if the weather was fine, the hauling was not. Lobsters were scarce, more so than was normal, even for July. In places where they had always done well, they were bringing up too many empty traps. When they shifted more gear onto the Triangle Ground, they did no better there than they had inshore.

"The Tates are hauling our gear," Petey said at least once every time out.

But Granddad was not ready to agree. He pointed to

the bait lines that were always tied with his knot.

"They could be pulling off a lath and taking the lobsters out that way," Petey said.

"Could be, but there's no sign they are."

"Maybe Spider has learned your knot. It isn't that hard."

Granddad shook his head. "Don't be so ready to blame poor hauls on thieving. Could be the lobsters just ain't crawling."

But when one of their pairs on the Triangle Ground disappeared and another one followed it a week later, Petey saw that Granddad knew what was happening. Yet he still seemed reluctant to do anything about it.

"They're going at us just the way they said they would," Petey told Granddad one afternoon. They were hauling on the Triangle Ground and had missed another pair.

"Maybe," Granddad said.

"We've got to stop them. We've got to cut off some of their traps."

"So they'll cut off more of ours? You know where that'll get us, don't you?"

"We can't let them push us around."

"We'll slow them up a bit." Granddad went to the wheel and guided the *Jenny and Susan* back and forth across the Triangle Ground. Each time they passed one of the Tates' glass toggles, he reached out with the gaff and broke it. "Now they'll know we're on to them."

But the broken toggles didn't stop the Tates. The price of lobsters jumped another dime, yet they weren't clearing as much money as they had cleared last summer. By the final week in July Petey's savings came to one hundred and sixty-five dollars.

He worked with Leo on the few foggy or windy days or whenever Granddad decided to let their traps set over an extra night. He rarely made much money. They turned down more jobs than they accepted.

A kind of blind hope kept him fighting for the *Wild Wind*. Each night before going to sleep, he put every dollar he could save into the pickle jar in his top bureau drawer.

They saw little of the Tates during all this time, except when they passed the *Pretty Lady* hauling. There were no more fights; the Tates kept out of their way, and try as he would, Petey could not spot them hauling any traps except their own. But Spider had plenty of chances. There was time early in the morning and in the evening, and Granddad's string was too large for them to keep watch over every trap even while they were out hauling.

As Petey had heard Spider tell the Wilson sisters, he and Danny weren't trying to drive Granddad into a corner. So far their plan was working perfectly. Granddad broke toggles and talked about the cold war while Petey watched his hope for the *Wild Wind* die day by day.

One afternoon when they came into Carl Julian's lobster car, the Tates were there ahead of them. Granddad tied up, and they waited while Julian weighed the Tates' three crates of lobsters.

"Got quite a haul there," Petey shouted at Spider. "You must be just about the smartest lobster catcher on the whole island."

"Smarter than you, kid," Spider shouted back.

Petey jumped up on the stern and stepped onto the car. Julian finished at the scales and glanced up. "They're doing real well, Petey. Spider's right on 'em."

"Not hard to do when you're hauling another man's gear as well as your own."

Julian began emptying the crates into the water within the car. "Better not start anything, Petey," he said gently. "If you've got a complaint, take it to the warden."

"Sure, a lot of good that would do with no proof."

Spider glared at him from his seat on an overturned punt. "Why don't you get back into your boat and shut up?"

"Go to hell."

"Petey, get over here," Granddad yelled.

He moved away slowly without taking his eyes off Spider. Danny dropped his broom and joined Spider on the car.

"That's enough!" Carl Julian told them. "You want to fight, go somewhere else."

Petey helped Granddad lift their two barrels of lobsters onto the car. One of the barrels was only half full. The Tates easily had a hundred pounds more than they did. There was no way of knowing how many of the Tates' lobsters had come from Granddad's traps. No way of knowing, but Petey could guess.

While they were bringing the barrels to the scales,

Petey saw Spider hide a grin behind hands cupped to light a cigarette. He dropped his barrel to stand there staring, for Spider's smile hit him harder than anything the man had said. He knew then that he had to do something.

The rest of the time the Tates were on the car with them, he didn't open his mouth.

On the way up the shore to Fox Cove, Petey thought out his plan. If he could get the outboard on the punt started, he wouldn't have to row, but he'd need gas and oil mixed up. He could steal the gas easily enough from the spare can Granddad kept under the stern next to the extra toggles. Leo would have a quart of oil in the truck. He would have to be sure Granddad and Gram were asleep before he started out. . . .

Granddad glanced at him several times from the wheel. Before he could become suspicious, Petey snapped out of his trance and began clowning around with the cowbell that they kept on a hook screwed into one of the deckhouse studs. He rang it in Granddad's ears until the old man ordered him to take the wheel and went back to the stern to smoke his corncob pipe.

When Petey went to his room that night, the quart of oil was already hidden in a clump of bushes near the cove. He didn't undress. Instead, he pulled on a sweatshirt and waited beside the window for the right time to leave.

The wind was dying, the night nearly calm. From his window he could see the stars above the cove. The early moon had set. Everything was going his way, and his heart beat hard with excitement.

Gram and Granddad went to bed. They talked a while, and the bed squeaked once or twice as they settled in. Then it was quiet except for the faint roar of waves breaking far down the shore. The night pulled at him to be off, but he waited until he heard Granddad snoring. Then he lifted out his screen and let himself down onto the roof of the entry.

He went around to the dooryard and took the flashlight from Granddad's car. On the quick run to the shore he retrieved the can of oil, then slipped and slid down the path to the pulley line. It was nearly high water, and he was able to bring the punt onto the rocks close to where he stood. He untied the painter and pushed off with one foot. Silently he paddled out to where the *Jenny and Susan* floated on her mooring.

It took him only a few minutes to mix gas and oil in a gallon jug and fill the outboard. But he had no intention of starting the motor so close to shore. He searched the platform until he found their rusty bait knife. Once in the punt, he crouched facing the bow and rowed out of the cove into East Bay.

As he crossed the bay, he looked up into the night. The stars burned sharp and clear like thousands of eyes watching him. He shivered despite his warm sweatshirt and the work of rowing. He listened to his oars cutting into the water, heard the creak of the oarlocks and the close, soft sound of his own breathing. He felt the knife tucked through his belt as if it were burning against his side.

Beyond Tragedy Bluff he stopped rowing and tried the outboard. After several pulls on the starter, the motor caught, roaring out suddenly into the quiet of the night. He sat on the stern seat to steer down the dark, unlighted shore.

He did not plan to go out to the Triangle Ground. It was too far and he would have to pass the Tates' cove on the way. It would be better to stay on this side of the Tates, just in case. . . .

He knew where many of their traps were. Inside Hundred Wreck Ledges he killed the engine and used the flashlight to locate a group of buoys. The first one was Granddad's—he could tell by the shape of the spindle. The next was Canada's. When he reached the third, he pulled it into the punt with one hand and held it in front of the light. It was a Tate buoy, red under the barnacles and slime.

With grim satisfaction he pulled the knife from his belt and stuck it into the seat. Then he hauled along on the dripping warp until he had gone beyond the first toggle. In a moment he had cut through the nylon. He threw the slack end clear and let the other run out through his fingers. That was one trap Spider and Danny would never see again.

He rowed on until he found another of the Tates' buoys. He cut this warp exactly as he had the first. Even at low water slack he doubted they would be able to reach the second toggle, should they spot it. Outside the Ledges he cut off six buoys, leaving the toggles. They would be able to recover these traps, and he meant them to. This first time was only a warning.

Farther down the shore he cut several more warps to make sure they got the message. Tomorrow they would haul, tomorrow they would know. He felt his stomach begin to cramp, but there was no way to undo what he had done.

"It will work," he whispered to himself. "They'll leave our gear alone now."

He started the outboard. The punt rolled gently as he headed around toward the bay. The air against his face was sweet with the smell of the water. But from the sky the stars glared down, and he knew God had seen him.

FOURTEEN

~~~~~~~~~~~~~~~~~~~~~~~~~~~~~~~~~~

Cutting Gear

The next morning when Granddad called him, Petey sat up long enough to answer, then fell asleep again. Gram had to shake him awake twice.

"What's the matter, Petey?" she asked the second time. "Don't you feel well?"

"I'm all right," he mumbled.

She waited at the door for him to move. "Petey."

"I'm coming, I'm coming." He forced himself over to the edge of his bed.

"Don't keep him waiting," Gram said gently.

He listened to her footsteps going down the stairs. He hadn't slept well; he had tossed about for hours. His eyes burned and his head ached and he felt sick to his stomach.

He dressed as slowly as he dared, but he could not put off forever facing Granddad. The worst part was knowing his guilt must show so plainly. They would both guess he had done something terrible.

When he went down, his stomach rolled over at the smell of the scrambled eggs steaming on his plate. He tried to eat, but he couldn't swallow.

"What's the matter with him?" he heard Granddad ask Gram.

"I think he's got this mess that's going around. Maybe he should stay in today."

"I'm all right," he told them. "Didn't sleep so good, that's all."

"A boy your age shouldn't have trouble sleeping." Gram walked over and felt his forehead. "You're warm, Petey, and you look flushed."

He could take the refuge she was offering. He could go back to bed and . . . He pulled his head away from her hand and bent over his coffee.

"Petey . . ."

"I'm fine. I want to go to haul. Look outside. I can't lie around in bed on a morning like this."

Granddad was staring at him. Petey forced himself to smile. It made his mouth ache, but they left him alone after that.

"Let's go," Granddad said when Gram had finished packing their lunch. Petey stood up.

"But he hasn't finished his eggs," Gram said.

"I can't wait all day," Granddad snapped. "If he isn't hungry, he isn't hungry."

They walked down to the cove. It was later than usual. Beads of dew on the tall grass sparkled in the light of the climbing sun.

"Hurry up, Petey!" Granddad shouted at him. He was waiting on the path ahead. "You didn't sneak out last night to see Sheila Wilson, did you?"

Petey shook his head.

Granddad led the way to the pulley line. Petey was

already sweating so hard he had to unbutton his outside shirt. They said nothing more to each other as Granddad rowed them out to the mooring.

They hauled in the bay and then along Seal Bar. Petey threw himself into the rhythm of the work, trying to lose himself in the bait and the lobsters and the traps rising from the green darkness of the water. For a while he could do this, until halfway to North Head when he caught himself looking down the length of the shore to see where the Tates were hauling. Squinting against the glare he saw the *Pretty Lady* off Hundred Wreck Ledges, and from then on there was no way to forget, no way to think of anything else.

"What's troubling you, Petey?" Granddad asked as they hauled their next trap. "You're all bound up in silence."

"Tired."

"Why?"

"No special reason."

Granddad pulled the turns from the winch head, and together they brought the trap from the water. It was empty, but they were used to this now. Petey reached for the bait needle.

"You know, if there's something wrong . . ." Granddad started to say. Petey could have taken this chance to tell him, but he didn't. The moment was gone as quickly as it had come, and a few seconds later the trap splashed down into the water again.

They shifted much of their gear from North Head to

Patience Shoal, and it was late in the morning before they ran down to Tragedy Bluff to resume hauling. The Tates were farther down the shore now, nearly out of sight below the Ledges.

Granddad had given up trying to talk to him. Each deep in his own thoughts, they worked side by side in silence, weaving through the day in the circle of their tasks.

By now, Petey knew, the Tates must have missed the traps and buoys he had cut off. He tried to watch them, but they were too far down the shore. He could feel the day around him hanging on a balance. He was helpless to force it either way.

They stopped to eat, then went on hauling. The hours of the afternoon passed slowly. For a while Canada and two other lobstermen hauled nearby, but the Tates were gone.

Below the Cut, Petey could look out and see the top of Triangle Rock through the smoky haze. The Tates might be hauling out there or they might be on their way to town to sell. Maybe cutting their gear had done the job. Maybe they were worried right now, afraid of what might happen if they continued to tamper with Granddad's traps.

Petey was filling up the second barrel. They had caught a few shedders, although none this far down the shore. Like a natural clock, the catching of lobsters that had formed new shells marked the passing of time, the advancing of summer and the coming of fall.

They were hauling their last traps below Bottomless Cove when Petey looked up and saw the *Pretty Lady* bearing down upon them from the direction of Triangle Rock.

"Now what do they want?" Granddad complained. He swung the *Jenny and Susan* away from the rocks and idled out into deeper water. Petey clenched his hands around the handle of the gaff. It was coming now and he had been waiting all day, and yet he knew he wasn't ready. He glanced at Granddad. The old man was pushing tobacco into his pipe in a good imitation of unconcern. Petey didn't know what to do. The time for explaining was gone.

The *Pretty Lady* rapidly closed the distance between them. Petey saw Spider peering around the side of his deckhouse. Danny was crouching by the stern and as his brother cut their speed, he picked up a buoy and threw it across the narrowing stretch of water separating the two boats. It landed on the platform behind Petey and bounced against the gas tank. It was one of Granddad's large buoys from the Triangle Ground.

Spider came to the side and waved his fist at them. "You want war, Shannon, that's what you're going to get!"

Granddad dropped his pipe onto the engine box. "What are you talking about, Spider?"

"Protecting my gear, that's what."

"By cutting off mine?"

Danny spit into the water. "You cut off a bunch of our traps last night! We know it was you. We got one by the toggle, and the warp was cut with a knife. You done it to us, damn you!"

Petey saw the puzzled anger on Granddad's face. If

only he had had the courage to tell Granddad before this, to warn him in time. If only he had explained. . . .

The *Pretty Lady* had drifted by. Spider went forward and shifted into reverse. As he swung the wheel he glared back at them. "Just remember, Shannon, you started it. And now you're going to get all you can handle."

"And then some!" Danny screamed.

"You're crazy," Granddad shouted back. "We never touched your gear."

Spider shook his head like a wounded animal. "Lying old man! I'll fight you till your last trap is gone. I'll drive you off the Triangle Ground and I'll drive you off the east side."

"Get out of here," Granddad told him. "You've been drinking too much of that rotten whisky."

As the *Pretty Lady* passed them in reverse, Danny started to jump across. Spider grabbed him by his oil pants and pulled him back. "See you around, old man."

Petey watched the *Pretty Lady* roar off, cutting around in a sharp arc to head down the shore toward town.

Granddad flipped off the belt with the end of the gaff, and the noisy winch head stopped turning. "We're going out to the Triangle Ground, but first I want to ask you something."

Petey looked at him for a moment, then at the rocks along the shore. They were drifting in, but Granddad didn't seem to notice.

"I want the truth, Petey." Granddad's voice was strained with patience. "I know they were drunk, but someone cut off those traps of theirs. Do you know who did it?"

Petey picked up a broken crab from the washboard and dropped it gently over the side. "Yes."

"Who was it?"

"Me. I had to. I couldn't let them go on stealing from us."

"You had no right," Granddad said.

Petey looked up at him. "You weren't doing a thing."

Granddad stared at him without blinking. "You had no right to take it on yourself to do anything at all."

"It's my money, too."

"Shut up." Granddad pointed to the wheel. "Take us out to the Triangle Ground."

Petey ran the *Jenny and Susan* out toward Triangle Rock under the sloping sky of late afternoon. He knew what Granddad was expecting. There was the white and black buoy behind him on the platform.

No other boats were in sight when they reached the Triangle Ground. Off to the northeast, gulls circled the empty stone ridges of Triangle Rock. Looking back through the haze, Petey thought even Hunter Island seemed ghostly and lifeless, as if when they returned there, they would find no one left.

It was hard to believe what had happened, except for the ache in his stomach that told Petey this was no bad dream. As they crisscrossed the Triangle Ground looking for their buoys, it slowly sank in that their traps were gone, cut off and out of their reach forever.

Granddad took the wheel and circled back, but it was pointless and they both knew it. Two or three other lobstermen had a few pairs each along the western edge. Everywhere else the Tates' red buoys marked the blue-gray water unchallenged.

Petey wanted to be angry, but he felt only a strange kind of fear, as if he had just discovered a deep hole beneath his feet. He could only look at the water and think about the forty-two traps they would never haul again.

"See what you've done?" Granddad yelled at him. He took hold of Petey's shirt and pushed him toward the side. "Look at it. Feast your eyes. Does it satisfy you?"

Petey tried to pull away from him, but Granddad's grip was too strong.

"Answer me!"

"I-I'm sorry."

Granddad twisted him around and slapped his face so hard Petey fell to the platform. "You're sorry! If I had anyone else, Petey, I'd put you ashore for good."

The thing that bothered him most was crying and having Granddad see him. Petey got to his feet quickly and went to stand by the stern looking away. He was too angry now to think of anything to say, but he swore to himself he would not apologize again. He heard the winch head begin turning. He looked around and Granddad saw his face.

"I'm going to do the only thing left to do," Granddad said. He put the engine in gear and headed for the nearest of the Tates' buoys.

Petey went over to the washboard and picked up the gaff, but Granddad snatched it out of his hands. "Go sit on the stern, boy. I'll do this by myself."

Petey shook his head and reached for the gaff. "I'm not a boy."

Granddad stared at him. For a moment Petey thought they would have to fight, and then, surprisingly, Granddad handed him the gaff.

"Do you know what it will be?"

Petey nodded.

They glided past the Tates' buoy to the toggle, and Petey reached out with his gaff. He hauled half the warp up on the winch, then held it for Granddad to cut with one quick slash of the bait knife. Petey threw the slack end of the warp overboard. In exactly this way they cut off every pair the Tates had on the Triangle Ground.

When they were done, Granddad kicked off the belt. He stared at Petey a moment, then looked away. "Let's go in and sell."

It was evening as they crossed the empty water toward Hunter Island. They did not speak again until they had to.

FIFTEEN

~~~~~~~~~~~~~~~~~~~~~~~~~~~~~~~~~~~~~~

"If I Was Married
to a Rich Man"

During the days following the cutting of the traps
on the Triangle Ground, Petey felt as if he was waiting
for the sky to fall. They hauled five days in a row during
a spell of hot and strangely windless weather. The Tates
hauled each day too. He and Granddad shifted some of
their inshore traps out onto the Triangle Ground, length-
ening out with three new coils of nylon. The Tates set
traps there the next day. Every day they hauled within
sight of each other. It was as if no one else existed, as if
all the hate between men everywhere was concentrated
between them.

"The Tates have had their fill," Granddad said one
afternoon as they hauled their new pairs on the Triangle
Ground.

Petey nodded, but he wondered how long this nervous truce would last.

He was spending a lot of his free time at the old house
with Leo, avoiding Granddad as much as possible. One
Friday evening when he planned to go to town, Leo
suggested he take Sheila to the movies.

"I don't know," Petey said.

122

"Well, you're going to," Leo told him, pushing him toward the truck. On the ride down Petey tried to look sure of himself. He had wanted to date Sheila all along, but lacked the courage to ask her. He wondered if Leo had guessed this.

"What if she won't come?"

"Why don't you wait and see." Leo pointed to the glove compartment. "There's a comb in there. Use it."

When they reached Sheila's house Leo drove in and stopped. "Go on. I'll turn around."

Petey dropped down to the ground and walked to the door. He looked back once, but Leo waved him on. He knocked and went in.

"Well hello there, Petey!" Ruth called. She was sitting at the kitchen table playing solitaire, a half-emptied glass of beer beside her right elbow, her hair up in curlers. She smiled at him expectantly.

"Is Sheila here?"

"I think she's in her room, Petey." Ruth stood up. "I'll get her. She'll be real pleased you've come."

While he waited alone in the kitchen, Petey looked out the back window toward the cove and tried to tell himself he wasn't blushing. He heard footsteps and turned around to see Sheila coming in alone. Over her shirt and blouse she was wearing a hip-length white sweater with flecks of silver thread woven in that sparkled faintly as she moved. She had her hair fixed so that it swept around from the left side of her face to tumble down her right shoulder.

"Hi, Petey. Ruth just told me you were here. How have you been?"

"Pretty good."

She was watching him closely. "Would you like to sit down?"

"No, Leo's outside. We . . . I thought you might like to go to the movie, unless you're busy tonight."

She smiled. "I'm not busy."

"Then you want to go?"

"I'd love to. I'll go tell Ruth."

He waited for her by the door. It had all happened so quickly and easily he was only beginning to realize she had been expecting him to come.

Sheila sat between them on the ride to town, but closer to Petey than to Leo. He could smell the scent of the soap she had used.

"I hope you like the picture," he told her. He made sure she was looking at his mouth. "It's that one about werewolves."

The movie was not a success. Halfway through, Sheila tugged on his arm and asked to leave. Once they were outside, he saw how pale she was.

"I'm sorry," he said. "I shouldn't have taken you to that one."

She shook her head. "It's my fault. I can't stand seeing someone get killed. I'll be all right."

She was upset and he knew it. "Let's go for a walk. We can buy Cokes down at Ellie's."

"I'd like that," she said.

The sun had set, but there was still enough light so that he could watch her as they walked. They bought their

Cokes in the grocery store by the parking lot, then drifted along Main Street.

"The big night in town," Sheila said, pointing to the crowded A&P. "I wonder what it would be like to live in a place where there are new things to do every night of the week."

"Be exciting, I guess."

"I'd love it. Especially if I was married to a rich man who could buy me everything I wanted. Dresses and shoes and a red sports car and even a poodle all my own. And we'd go out every night to a different restaurant and . . ."

"Who? You and the poodle?"

"Oh Petey, stop it. I'm serious."

"I wouldn't want to leave Hunter Island."

"What?"

He repeated his words more slowly.

"It's getting dark," she said. "Come on. I want to show you something."

She took him up the steep sidewalk on Signal Hill. Near the top, along one side of the street, there were three stores that opened only for the summer season. Sheila stopped in front of Daisy's Dress Shop.

"See, isn't it pretty?"

She was pointing at a yellow, sleeveless dress in Daisy's front window.

"Don't you like it?"

Petey nodded. "It's nice."

"Buy it for me, Petey?"

He looked at her excited face in the light of the shop window. "I don't know."

"I've wanted it so long," she said. "It's just my size. Don't you think it would look nice on me?"

He nodded. "But she's probably closed, and . . ."

"No she isn't, Petey Shannon. She stays open until nine-thirty on Friday nights. See? All the lights are on inside."

"I need my money to buy the *Wild Wind.*" He didn't like the defensive sound in his voice.

"If a boy cares about a girl, he buys her pretty things."

"Yeah, I suppose."

"There's only one left and if you don't buy it for me, some other girl will get it."

Petey shifted his weight onto his right foot and looked down the street.

"But you won't buy it for me, will you?"

He shook his head. "I've got to save my money."

"Petey, I hate you."

"Want to walk around some more?"

She studied his mouth in the window light. "No, I guess not, Petey. I'd better be getting home."

He walked unhappily down the hill beside her. He could feel her angry resentment in the way she walked apart, refusing to look at him. There was no chance for him to talk to her unless she chose to let him.

The truck was in the parking lot. "Leo said he'd be over to the Half Tide," he told her. "I'll go get him."

She didn't say anything, and he wasn't sure she had been able to read his lips. When he started to walk across the parking lot she ran after him.

"Don't be angry with me."

He turned to face her. "I'm not."

"I'm sorry I was so awful. Forgive me?"

"Sure."

She put her arms around his waist and squeezed him for a moment. "I'll wait here." She kissed his chin before letting him go.

The Half Tide was crowded. Petey pushed through the tangle of arms and legs, avoided the Tates and forced his way into the back room where two games were going at once. Leo was playing at the first table with Canada and four other lobstermen. When Petey tapped his shoulder, he nearly jumped out of his chair.

"Don't bother me now."

"We're ready to go."

"This early?"

"Yeah."

Leo gathered up the cards and began to shuffle them. "One more hand."

Petey stood there waiting while Leo played three more hands of stud, winning enough in the last pot to put him a few dollars ahead. He nodded to the other men and got up from his chair.

"I'll be back. Got to drive the kid's girl home."

"Let him take the truck," one of the men suggested. "He can drive, can't he?"

Petey thought this was a great idea, but Leo shook his head. "He hasn't got his license yet. And you know Coughlin. He always patrols on Friday nights. Be just my luck to have him catch the kid and put the blame on me."

On the way out Petey's hand brushed against his back pocket. "My wallet's gone!"

They squeezed out to the street. "Maybe you dropped it in the truck."

Petey shook his head. "I had it when I bought the movie tickets."

They crossed to the parking lot. "Well, think a minute," Leo told him. "Did you have it out anywhere else?"

"No. I paid for our Cokes with some change. Someone could have taken it from my pocket in the poolroom."

"Could have, but nobody around here is a pickpocket, far as I know. Where's Sheila?"

Petey looked up into the cab of the truck. It was empty. He walked around in a full circle, but Sheila was nowhere in sight. "She said she'd wait here."

"What's the matter?" Leo asked.

"We had a little fight and . . ."

"Where are you going?"

"Got to check something," Petey shouted. He ran across the parking lot, jumped the low stone barrier and raced along Main Street. By the time he had climbed the hill to Daisy's Dress Shop, he was breathing too hard to talk. He shot into the store just as Daisy was closing the blinds in the front window.

"Are you looking for Sheila Wilson?" Daisy asked. She didn't seem too surprised to see him. Beneath a puff of white hair her large gray eyes studied him intently. "You're Peter Shannon, aren't you?"

He nodded.

Daisy crossed to the main counter and picked up his wallet. "This is yours then. She said you would be in after it."

He took it and checked his money. He had made fourteen dollars today. There was only one dollar left now.

Daisy was still staring at him. "I don't really know what this is all about."

"Did she buy the yellow dress?" Petey tried to wipe away the sweat running down his forehead.

"Yes, she did. And a two-and-a-half-dollar blouse. She started out after she made her purchases, then she came back and handed me your wallet and told me to please keep it for you, that she thought you would come for it. I tried to make her explain, but she ran out before I could more than open my mouth."

He put the wallet into his pocket.

"Should I have stopped her? But I didn't realize that . . ."

"It's all right."

Daisy walked with him to the door. "I've got to close now. Are you and Sheila going together?"

"Sort of," Petey said. He thanked her and walked down the hill. He knew it was useless, yet he looked around as he walked in case Sheila was still close by. But in the deserted streets, he saw nothing moving at all.

On the ride home later that night, Leo pried the truth out of him. Petey was feeling more ashamed than angry, and he didn't want to talk about what Sheila had done, but Leo wouldn't let up until he had the whole story.

He burst into taunting laughter as they rattled over the dark and dusty road. "Took you for your roll, hey Petey? That's the best one yet. I'll treasure it for years."

"Shut up."

"I don't see why you didn't buy her the dress in the first place. A girl like Sheila wants to be taken care of.

Trouble with you is you're tight. Squeeze every dollar
you make until it squeals."

"Why don't you . . ."

"Easy now, boy. I'm your uncle, so don't go losing your
head."

It seemed to Petey that Leo was steering on purpose
to hit every bump in the road. And after each jolt, he
cackled louder than he had on the one before.

Petey thought about Sheila often. During the hauling, during the trips down around to sell, during the
nights before sleep, he went over everything that had
happened on their date. He repeated to himself everything she had said and remembered every move she had
made.

He began to hate himself for not doing the gallant
thing. If he had bought her the dress, it would be so easy
to go see her again. But now, the way it was, he didn't
know what to do.

Lobsters went for two prices, as more and more shedders were caught. The bigger hauls brought in more
money. He saved all he could, but Gram made him buy
some school clothes and half of August was gone before
he had two hundred and fifty dollars put away.

It was Gram who found out about his date with Sheila.
She came upstairs one evening while he was in his room
clipping his nails with a pair of wire cutters. As soon as
she walked in, he knew he was going to be lectured.

"Are you seeing the Wilson girl?" she asked him.

He glanced up at her. "Why?"

"I heard you took her to the movie last week."

"Who told you?"

"Never mind who told me. I heard it from more than one person, as a matter of fact."

"So?"

"Didn't your grandfather tell you to stay away from her?"

"Yeah."

"But you disobeyed." She sat down in the chair near the window. "What's come over you, Petey? Ever since you got wrapped up in this plan to buy back your father's boat, you haven't been yourself at all."

He shrugged.

"You're not serious about Sheila, are you?"

"What if I was?"

Gram stared at him. "You're too young. Besides, she's the wrong kind of girl."

He got up off his bed and walked out of the room.

"Petey?"

"I'm going down to see Leo."

"You come back here right now. I'm not through."

Granddad tried to stop him in the kitchen. Petey ducked by and ran out through the entry. He heard Granddad yell something at Gram, but he didn't try to listen. He no longer cared what they thought about him.

SIXTEEN

~~~~~~

The Exalted Order of
Eastern Indians Hall Dance

On the few days they let their traps set over, Petey worked with Leo. The long stretch of hot weather was giving the garbage business a special taint, and Leo needed all the help he could get.

They were removing a week's collection of boxes and spoiled produce from a shed behind the Shallow Harbor grocery store when Leo pointed up the road. "Here comes your sweetheart."

Petey straightened up and looked over the side of the truck. A white convertible turned the corner by the store and drove off toward town, but not before he saw Sheila sitting in front beside the boy who was driving. Her sisters were in back with two other boys.

"Was that Clyde Anderson?" Petey asked.

"Yeah, with two of his buddies from college. Nice car. Guess they're taking the girls for a swim."

Petey wasn't sure if the sneer in Leo's voice was aimed at him or at the summer boys. He leaned against the sideboard.

"Don't worry," Leo yelled from the shed. "I don't think she saw you." A rotten plum splashed off Petey's

132

shoulder. "Get to work. You're holding up progress here."

Petey went back to stacking boxes in the body of the truck. But for the rest of the afternoon he thought about Sheila with those summer boys. Clyde Anderson's father was rich. Clyde could buy Sheila anything she wanted. Leo guessed what was bothering him and teased him unmercifully. "You had your chance, kid," he told him, "and you blew it. Don't cry now. You can't operate like those college boys, anyway."

At the dump Petey retaliated by throwing a shovelful of coffee grounds into Leo's face. It didn't make him feel any better, not even when they traded punches.

The next day he and Granddad had their biggest haul since the spring spurt. Granddad's stomach was bothering him again. He ran the boat and left most of the actual hauling to Petey. When they came into the harbor, they saw the *Wild Wind* far down at the bow.

"Deven's going to let her sink right here in the harbor," Petey said. "Put me on board and I'll pump her out."

"Let him tend to it," Granddad said.

But Petey talked him into landing him on the boat, and while Granddad went off to sell their lobsters and gas up, Petey pumped out bucketful after bucketful of bilge water with the rusty hand pump Mr. Deven kept on board. The undertaker rowed out in his punt before he was done.

"She had water six inches over the planks up forward," Petey told him, handing him the pump.

Mr. Deven stared at him. "You don't own her yet,

Petey. Suppose you wait until you do before you start throwing your weight around."

Petey swallowed hard. "Granddad's going to pick me up." He sat down on the stern deck and watched Mr. Deven slowly pumping water into the bucket. At the rate he was going, the *Wild Wind* would probably sink first.

"How are you coming with the money," Mr. Deven called back to him.

"Don't worry," Petey told him. "I'll have it in time." And he would take the boat away from Deven then and never let a man like him on board again.

"I've got to haul a load of slabs from Cricket's sawmill to the Gilmore place," Leo told him over a supper of canned beans and hot dogs. "Want to help? Might be a few dollars in it for you."

"Sure." Petey washed down the last piece of overcooked hot dog with half a glass of water. "I'm ready."

They took the truck across the island to the sawmill and piled it high with spruce slabs, then delivered the load at the Gilmores' huge summer house on West Bluff. Ten dollars richer, hot and sweaty, they struck out for town from there.

On Main Street they tangled in the busiest traffic of the year. "There's going to be a good crowd at the dance tonight," Leo said. "Look at all those cars."

They stopped for gas at Mel Swift's garage, then found a place to leave the truck in the back of the parking lot. As they walked across the lot toward the Half Tide Pool

Room, Petey glanced up at the brightly lit hall above the A&P.

"I forgot they were having a dance tonight."

Leo grunted. "Weren't planning to go anyway, were you?"

"No."

"Might be some nice-looking girls there. Maybe you should go in and take a look."

"No."

They were nearing the street when Petey saw Sheila getting out of Clyde Anderson's white convertible. She was wearing the yellow dress. They stared at each other as he and Leo walked closer. Petey wanted to say hello, but his mouth wouldn't open.

"Hey Clyde," Leo shouted. "That's some hunk of tin. Must have set your old man back something."

Clyde nodded at them but didn't speak. He was thickset and muscular, and Petey remembered hearing somewhere that he played football at college. In the glare of the parking lot lights his broad, tanned face looked like a handsome mask, stiff and lifeless below his slightly disarranged blond curls. He was dressed perfectly in a blue blazer and tan, sharply creased trousers that made Petey suddenly conscious of his own dirty work clothes.

"Hi Petey," Sheila said. "Aren't you coming to the dance?"

He shook his head. "Forgot all about it."

She was trying to read his lips, and he said it again more slowly. There was a look on her face he didn't understand. He wondered if she was afraid of him because she had stolen his money to buy the dress she was wearing.

"You look nice," he said, but Clyde was already moving her away from them and he didn't think she had caught his words. He watched her walk toward the entrance to the hall with Clyde beside her. There was an angry taste in his mouth.

"Why don't you go?" Leo said. "All I'm planning on is a little poker. I'll give you your share from the money Gilmore paid me."

"No, I can't. I'm not even dressed decent."

"Who cares? If you washed up when you came in from hauling, you're way ahead of half those clowns going in there right now."

"Yeah, but I look lousy." Petey hurried across the street to the Half Tide. Leo caught up with him, and they went inside.

"Who are you kidding, Petey?" Leo demanded. "You're eating your heart out over that girl. I saw the way you looked at her. Why don't you do something about it?"

Petey smiled at him. "I'm going to play some pool with old Cud, that's what I'm going to do."

He walked over to one of the racks on the far wall and selected a cue. Leo watched him a moment, then shrugged his shoulders in disgust and went into the back room.

The Half Tide wasn't crowded, and Cud Baxter was able to play several games of eight ball with him without interruption.

"How come the Tates aren't in tonight?" Petey asked.

Cud shoved a stick of gum into his mouth and casually lined up a shot. "Over to the dance."

"The Tates?"

"Yeah. Told me they were going to have some fun tonight for a change. Made a crack as how playing on my tables was more like work. I told them there wasn't no law says they got to come in here every night."

Cud went on about the Tates, but Petey paid little attention. He was losing, missing shots any kid half his age would have made.

"Guess this ain't your night," Cud said as he sank the eight ball to end the fourth game. "That's forty cents you owe me."

There was a burst of laughter from the card room. Petey looked in and saw that Leo had just won a big pot. He put up his cue and went back to get his money. Leo gave him four dollars as his share for hauling the slabs.

"That enough?"

"Yes sir."

"Where you headed?"

"Across the street."

Leo smiled. "Behave yourself now."

Petey nodded and walked out front where he paid Cud the forty cents he owed him for the four games of eight ball he had lost.

"Evening's young yet, Petey," Cud said. "Let's play some more."

"Can't."

Out on the street he could hear music from the dance rolling out through the open windows of the Exalted Order of Eastern Indians Hall. As he crossed the street, he ran his fingers through his hair in an effort to smooth it down, although he knew there wasn't much point in worrying about his hair, not the way he was dressed. But he was going to that dance. He wasn't going to run off somewhere and hate himself.

He climbed the stairs to the third floor of the building and bought his ticket. The hall inside was crowded with people standing around in groups. Along the left side of the barnlike room a few of the older women were sitting on folding chairs. On the other side, under crepe paper streamers, tables had been set up in an imitation of an outdoor café. Petey saw Sheila sitting at one of these tables with Clyde.

For a while he stood in a dark corner with the other boys who had no dates. Around him they smoked their hidden cigarettes and told dirty jokes, but he kept his eyes on Sheila as she danced with Clyde. She kept time with him perfectly, and Petey wondered how she did it.

The music dominated the hall. Seth Alfred had his electric guitar turned up too loud. He sat with his back to the others, gazing out one of the windows into the night. Skinny Hegman was pounding the keys of the piano, a wide grin on his face as he shook his head in time to his playing. Teddy Parsons and his wife Claire were watching the dancers as they wove the melody in and out with their saxophones.

Near Sheila and Clyde he saw Spider Tate dancing with Sheila's sister Barbie. He didn't see Ruth, but Danny Tate was in a corner by himself doing a clog dance in his fishing boots.

With each number more couples stepped out onto the

floor, and the building began to shake. When Clyde left Sheila at their table and walked out front toward the refreshments, Petey threaded his way quickly through the crowd and touched her arm.

"If the next one is slow, will you dance with me?"

She gave him a strange, unsmiling look but nodded, and when the band started playing something slow, he took her in his arms and they moved toward the dance floor. He wasn't very good, but somehow she seemed to make him better than usual.

"They're out of practice," she said with a faint smile, nodding toward the band.

"How do you . . ." he started to ask.

"I can hear music a little, if it's loud enough. And I feel it, sort of inside me."

When he said nothing more, she glanced around at the tables. "He sees us and he's jealous."

Petey looked over and saw Clyde scowling at them. Petey knew this dance was nearly over. "You're pretty in that dress," he told Sheila.

She looked pleased. "And you're not angry?"

"No."

"I thought you'd be. I thought you would hate me."

"I don't."

The music stopped. Reluctantly he walked her back to her table. She turned near her chair and smiled at him. "Thank you, Petey."

Clyde was staring at him. "See you around, kid. Thanks for taking care of my date for me."

Sheila was already drinking her Coke. As Petey turned and walked away, he heard Clyde say something to

Sheila. It was lost in the noise, and then he was being pressed toward the stag corner by a group of newly arrived summer people.

As the evening passed, he danced with Sheila three more times. He waited for her to say something—anything that would tell him she wanted to break off with Clyde. But she spoke only of small and unimportant things, like the things he talked about, and watched him with a kind of smile that grew more and more scornful as time passed. During a dance after the eleven o'clock intermission she began to tease him about his clumsiness, and when he took her back to Clyde, she told him she wouldn't dance with him again.

"Why?"

She shook her head. "I'm here with Clyde. He asked me, not you."

Clyde grinned at him. "Besides, you're no Fred Astaire."

Petey tried to ignore him. "What's wrong, Sheila?"

She looked at him coldly. "Don't you know?"

He wanted to say yes he did know and he would do whatever he had to do to make things right, but he knew nothing at all. His puzzled look only made Sheila angry.

"Go away, Petey."

Clyde stood up. He was taller than Petey with a look of maturity Petey knew he could not match. "Get lost, will you?"

Petey hesitated.

"Go on, Petey," Sheila said. "Stop hanging around like

a lost puppy." She reached over and touched Clyde's arm. "Take me for a ride, please, honey?"

Clyde nodded, and Petey watched them walk off toward the exit. Sheila turned and looked back when they were halfway across the floor. He realized with a shock that she was crying.

Then he understood what he had done wrong, and he plunged into the crowd, trying to reach her before she left. As the music started, people in couples and groups reeled out toward the center of the hall. By the time he had broken through the crowd and run to the stairs, Sheila and Clyde were gone.

As he raced down the stairs, he was suddenly hearing Leo's voice in his mind, telling him that Sheila needed someone to take care of her. He swung himself over a landing and onto the next flight of stairs. Like a fool he had waited for her to say something when all along she had been waiting for him to make his claim on her. She had teased and taunted him, trying to make him angry enough to show his real feelings toward her. But only when he had seen her looking back, tears running down her face, had he finally understood.

By the time he reached the parking lot, they were already driving out in Clyde's white convertible. He waited to see which direction they took, then ran to the back of the lot to get Leo's truck. The key was in the ignition, and there was no time to ask Leo. Petey roared onto Main Street and turned left.

He had seen Clyde drive past Shallow Harbor Road and down Main Street. Although the convertible was now out of sight, Petey didn't think Clyde had turned off on East Bay Road. Petey had to make up his mind one way or the other. He headed out of town on East Main Street.

It made sense. East Main Street became a dirt road three miles out, but it continued on for several more miles past some of the wealthiest summer homes on the island, including the Andersons' stone mansion at Apple Hill. If Clyde didn't take Sheila there, he would probably drive on to Lookout Beach. This was the usual place to take a girl; it was small and secluded, yet easy to reach by car.

He drove as fast as he dared, but reached the end of the tarred road without seeing the convertible. Doubts began to eat at him then. What if Clyde had turned up East Bay Road after all? He could never double back now and find him. No, Clyde was a fast driver; he was somewhere up ahead.

When Petey saw the Andersons' house, he slowed down, but there were no lights showing in the windows and only a black sedan in the driveway. He stepped hard on the gas and roared on toward Lookout Beach. Thoughts of Sheila kept flashing through his mind—all the chances he had missed, all the times he had been afraid to make his move.

He nearly drove by the turnoff for the beach, he was so deep in his thoughts. He slammed on the brakes and skidded onto the sandy track that twisted down through the junipers and scrub spruce. The left front wheel hit a stump, but he held on all the way to the beach, where his headlights picked up Clyde's car parked only a hundred feet away. He switched off the engine and lights and jumped down to the sand.

He was running forward the moment he hit the sand, for already he could see that Clyde was backing around to leave. He felt a wild happiness as his feet pounded over the hard sand, and when he reached the convertible, he opened the door and pulled Clyde out in one rough, confident motion.

"Come on, Sheila," he shouted. "You're going with me. You're my girl."

He could dimly see her face in the green lights of the dash. She didn't move, and then he realized that dark as it was, she couldn't understand a word he was saying.

SEVENTEEN

~~~~~~~~~~~~~~~~~~~~~~~~~~~~~~~~

Time Running Out

He heard a grunt just before Clyde's fist rammed into his neck. He fell back onto the sand, twisted around and grabbed Clyde's legs, bringing him down, too. For a moment he had the advantage, but the other boy's weight and strength were too much for him. He tried to stand up, but Clyde forced him down and pinned him against some rocks where Petey couldn't fight off the fists that Clyde drove into his face.

Sheila was begging them to stop. Petey slashed out with his knees and elbows and managed to loosen Clyde's weight long enough to push himself out from under. Still in a crouch he threw his right fist as hard as he could in the direction of Clyde's bobbing face. He felt the jolt as his punch landed. Clyde ducked to one side. Petey never saw the kick that caught him in the stomach.

It was all over then and he knew it, even as he dropped openmouthed onto the sand. Somewhere far off he could hear Sheila screaming at Clyde. He fought against the rising sickness in his stomach. He told himself over and over to get up, find Sheila, and take her away from Clyde.

144

He heard the convertible roar, saw its headlights sweep across the scrub spruce as it turned to leave the beach. He pulled himself up onto his feet and lunged after the car, but he was too late. He watched the headlights flicker and go, heard the tires dig onto the hard dirt of the road.

"Petey."

He turned around and saw Sheila standing by the rocks. He walked over to her, still unsteady, with an ache in his middle that made it impossible for him to stand up straight. In the dark he saw her face only faintly and her hands as they moved together nervously.

"I hit him with a piece of driftwood and he . . . Petey, I'm sorry!"

She trembled within his arms the way a bird he had once caught had fluttered in his hands. He thought she was going to cry, but she didn't.

He took her over to a large boulder and made her sit down. There was a fire in his stomach that wouldn't go out, but he was more concerned with her than with himself. He traced a question mark on her arm. When she shook her head, he traced it again.

"I'm okay, Petey," she said with a small, nervous laugh. "He only kissed me." She reached out and touched his face. "You're bleeding."

He shrugged.

"No. Do you have a handkerchief?"

She kept her hand on his face while he nodded. "Go down to the water and wash out the cuts. They're all full of sand." When he didn't move, she pushed him away. "Go on now, Petey. Do it."

He walked down to the edge of the water, soaked his

handkerchief and cleaned up his face as best he could. Behind him he could hear her crying softly as if she was trying to hold it back. But in the still night he heard her clearly.

When he returned, she kissed him. "Why didn't you stop me sooner?" she asked, her words blurring together. "I only went out with him to make you jealous because you never came to see me again. Oh Petey, you're so thick. I only meant to make you look at me and want me enough to care about me and stop me."

He traced three words on the skin of her arm.

"Do it again."

He knew she had understood. "I love you," he said as he traced the words a second time.

Sheila kissed him and whispered in his ear. Behind them the small waves ran up on the beach, splashing a slow clock beat through the silence of the night.

Petey saw a lot of Sheila after that night on the beach. When Gram and Granddad tried to force him to stop meeting her, he brought her to the house one night so that they had to see her as she really was. Her shy nervousness took them by surprise and won them over quickly. As he had hoped, they could not remain hostile when she so obviously wanted them to like her and feared they wouldn't. Gram flew about, feeding them all too much coffee and pie, while Granddad dug out his collection of old photographs of the quarrying days and beamed when Sheila was properly impressed with pictures of his father.

Out to haul, he and Granddad kept a careful watch in

case of new trouble from the Tates. What had happened on the Triangle Ground wasn't forgotten. Both boats were tending large strings out there now, and as the lobstering improved, the tension seemed to grow, not lessen.

On the evening before the last day in August, Petey rode down with Leo and met Sheila in town. As they walked along Main Street, he saw Mr. Deven coming out of the paper store. When they passed, Petey stopped him and tried to talk the undertaker into giving him an extension beyond the September first deadline.

"I can't do it, Petey."

"Why? What difference will a few days make?"

Mr. Deven shook his head. "Our agreement on the *Wild Wind* stands. You're to have the money to me by twelve noon on the first, otherwise the deal is off."

"One more day?"

"No."

Petey thought he was hiding something behind his narrow smile. "Has someone else asked about her?"

"Maybe."

"Who?"

"The Tates."

Petey stared at him.

"The Tates have offered me six hundred dollars for her, so you can see why . . ."

"I'll get the money to you," Petey cut in.

"Good, Petey. I'll be looking for you day after tomorrow."

Sheila took his hand as they walked away. "He's a terrible man, Petey. He was laughing at you all the time you were talking." She shivered and leaned against his arm.

"I'm still ninety dollars short," he said suddenly, then felt immediately ashamed of his weakness.

"What?"

He shook his head, but she cupped his chin in her hand and brought his face toward hers.

"Tell me."

"I have only three hundred and ninety dollars saved. I need ninety more and there's only one day left."

She nodded in understanding but said nothing until they stopped by a bench in front of the library. "Petey, you won't do anything bad, will you?" She was watching his lips closely.

"What do you mean?"

"I mean if you don't make the money in time and the Tates buy the *Wild Wind.*"

He sat down on the bench and pulled her down beside him.

"Petey, answer me."

The thought of the Tates taking Dad's boat made him sick. He looked up the street at a group of wild kids playing tag. "I don't know."

He wasn't facing her. She dug her nails into his arm. "Petey, tell me what you'll do."

He looked at her and shook his head. "They'll never get the *Wild Wind.*"

He didn't know if she had caught the meaning behind his words. She stared at him as if she was waiting for him to say something more.

"What do you want to do tonight?" he asked.

She didn't smile. "You tell me."

"The movie."

She stood up. "All right."

They walked back through town. Sheila seemed far away, and he asked her what she was thinking.

"Nothing."

"Are you worried about me?"

She tossed back her hair. "Why should I tell you if I am?"

When he and Leo took Sheila home in the truck, she leaned against him with her head on his chest, and he put his face into her hair. Leo said nothing as he drove. He waited in the truck while Petey walked Sheila to her door.

"I had a good time," she whispered as she turned to let him kiss her.

Around them the night was filled with the sound of waves beating steadily on the ledges offshore. When he kissed her, she held onto him a moment.

"Be careful tomorrow," she said.

He nodded. They stood together a while, neither of them wanting to say good-night but not able to talk well in the dark. Then quickly she reached up and touched his mouth with her hand.

"Good luck, Petey."

She went inside and he walked back to the truck. Leo kicked open the door.

"Rough out there tonight. Canada said something about a storm going by out to sea."

"Yeah." Petey turned and felt the air. A chill east wind was blowing.

EIGHTEEN

~~~~~~

"You Can't Haul Alone"

By morning the east wind was no stronger, but there was a peculiar, swollen look to the clouds that raced across the pale dawn sky.

"I don't know," Granddad said as he kicked the living room radio. "Doesn't look so good. We'd better get a forecast."

Petey stood in the kitchen doorway drinking his hot coffee. He watched Granddad turn the dial on the radio with the care of a safecracker. They had to go out today. The wind wasn't that bad. They had to haul. . . .

At last Granddad was able to tune in the Grant Harbor station. After the news the announcer read the weather forecast. When the commercial for Simon's Chicken Feed began, Granddad switched off the radio and walked past Petey into the kitchen.

"What did he say?" Gram asked.

"Variable winds going around to the northwest. There's a high pressure area coming down from Canada." Granddad poured himself another cup of coffee. "Not a word about that storm to the south'ard they were talking about last night."

"Must have gone out to sea," Petey said.

Granddad grunted. "Never noticed the Weather Bureau issuing any guarantees with their forecasts, have you?"

Petey laughed nervously. "We're going to haul, aren't we?"

Granddad walked to the window and looked up at the sky. "Damned funny. Reminds me of that time a while back."

"What time?"

"Years ago. Storm offshore and a big Canadian high coming down. Blew a screeching gale that day. Sunk half a dozen trawlers. They called it a tight pressure gradient between the high and the offshore storm."

"Wasn't anything like that in this morning's forecast."

Granddad turned away from the window. "They didn't say anything about it that time either, till afterwards."

They drank their coffee slowly. Granddad seemed to be waiting for something to make up his mind for him.

Petey couldn't finish his second cup. "Granddad, we have to haul today. Tomorrow's the first day of September."

"We can haul tomorrow."

"There won't be enough time. I have to give the money to Deven by twelve noon."

Granddad went to the bathroom, then came back and began hunting around for one of his pipes. "Go ahead, Jenny. Pack us a lunch. We'll give it a try."

The sun was shining between the clouds when they walked down the path to the pulley line, but the chop coming in from East Bay slapped noisily against the rocks. They went out and began hauling their pots in the bay itself, and it wasn't bad at all, even when the clouds thickened and a few drops of rain splashed down. Petey began to hope for a full day's haul as he put the hard lobsters into a bushel basket and the shedders into the first barrel.

"Wind's letting go a little," he said. They were working their way out toward the mouth of the bay.

Granddad shook his head. "No it's not. Shifting to the nor'ard."

When they left the shelter of the bay to haul their traps off Tragedy Bluff, the full force of the northeast wind struck them. The *Jenny and Susan* rolled through the confusion of short, choppy waves, then rose suddenly to meet a swell sweeping up the shore from the south. Petey, standing by the winch head with the gaff, had to grab the deckhouse roof to keep from falling over backwards.

"There's a real sea running under this mess," Granddad shouted from the wheel. He took the *Jenny and Susan* down to the lower end of their first string. When he swung around to come up beside the first buoy, Petey leaned out to gaff it only to have the boat roll with him, plunging his arm deep into the cold water. He made a second snatch with the gaff, caught the warp in front of the buoy and brought it in quickly.

The boat wallowed back as a sharp wave slapped off her side. Petey shook the water from his face and hair and put the turns on the winch head.

"Throw her clear!"

Petey looked at Granddad.

"You heard me. We can't haul in this. Throw that buoy overboard."

When Petey hesitated, Granddad waved his arm angrily. "Do as I say! Get that slack up fast!"

Petey took the turns from the winch, hauled in the slack warp, then scaled it out again as Granddad turned the *Jenny and Susan* away from the bluff. The white foaming water sparkled momentarily as the sun broke through the clouds. A gust of wind blew spray against the deckhouse windows. The *Jenny and Susan* reared up to meet the jagged sea.

"We're going in," Granddad told him when Petey moved to the shelter of the deckhouse. "It's going to blow a gale before it's through."

Petey hung onto the edge of the roof as Granddad ran the boat into the wind until they were well out from Tragedy Bluff. Petey felt a swelling disappointment. They were giving up, going in, failing. He was failing. . . .

Granddad turned the *Jenny and Susan* toward the entrance to the bay. With the wind and chop on their starboard side they rolled badly until they reached more sheltered water. Heavy gray clouds hid the sun again.

Granddad glanced sideways at him. "Sorry, Petey, but there's no real chance out there today. It's only going to get worse. Believe me, I know the signs."

Petey said nothing as they passed Parsons Ledge heading for the cove. There was no point in speaking, no point in arguing. And yet he felt none of the letting go inside him that he thought should come with defeat.

He walked to the stern and stood there braced tensely against the motion of the boat. A stream of sunlight parted the filthy gray clouds and touched the water out where the waves stood on end beyond the mouth of the bay. This slanting pillar of light seemed to measure the height of the sky that arched enormously above them.

He tried to think. He had been out there, off Tragedy Bluff—one of the roughest places on the whole east side. He had gaffed the buoy and he could have hauled the trap. He could have gone on hauling. . . .

"Petey."

Turning he saw that they were entering the cove. He stepped up onto the washboard, took the gaff and walked onto the bow, where he plucked the mooring buoy out of the punt as Granddad reversed the engine.

The wind here in the cove, deflected by the land, washed through the tops of the spruce trees. Petey glanced up at the swaying branches. If he gave up now, would he stop caring, or would the angry ache inside him just go on building?

He finished on the bow and brought the punt back, tying it over the winch head. Granddad had shut off the engine and was crating their lobsters, hard ones and shedders together.

"We can take these down and sell if you want," he said.

Petey shook his head. "No sense. Wouldn't be enough money there to do any good."

Granddad looked angry. "Don't blame me."

"I don't."

Granddad pushed the crate overboard and tied it to

the ringbolt in the stern deck. When they were ready to go, Petey held the punt for him, then climbed in and took the oars. He paid careful attention to his rowing. The moment they had scraped onto the rocks, Granddad stepped out with the painter in his hand.

"Hey, what did you do, Petey? Forget to bring the dinner pail?"

Petey looked around the punt. "Yeah, guess I did."

"Well go out and get it. No sense leaving good food to spoil."

Petey nodded and rowed out into the cove again. For just a moment he looked up and saw Granddad climbing onto the path. He suddenly wanted to call out and tell him the truth, that he had left the dinner pail aboard on purpose, but he said nothing. When he reached the *Jenny and Susan* Granddad was out of sight on the way to the house.

He worked quickly then, and by the time Granddad missed him and came back to find out what was wrong, Petey had the crate of lobsters on board again and was up on the bow tying the punt to the mooring pennant. Granddad shouted to him from the shore. Petey stood up straight.

"I'm going back out there to haul, Granddad," he called to him across the cove.

"Don't be a little fool, Petey!" Granddad shouted. "You can't haul alone. You'll be drowned."

Petey left the bow and swung down under the house.

"Petey! Get in here. Get the hell off that boat!"

Petey didn't want to argue, but he wanted Granddad to understand. "I can't come in," he shouted. "I can't let the Tates buy the *Wild Wind.* I'm going out to get the money I need. I'll give you half of what I make. I've got to have the rest."

He could feel Granddad's rage all the way across the cove. Petey tore himself free. There was only one way to do this thing and that was to shut up and do it. He started the engine, then hurried to the bow to cast off. Granddad was shouting again, but the noise of the engine blocked out his words.

On the way out Petey quickly separated the lobsters again, putting the hard ones in one barrel, the shedders into the other. As he pulled on his oil pants, he looked back. He expected Granddad to shake his fist at him, to walk out along the path, to do something. But until the tip of Rocky Point came between them, the old man just stood there watching him go.

NINETEEN

~~~~~~

"What if You Wasn't to Live till Tomorrow"

The fear was strange, like a sharp cut through the middle of his body. Standing at the wheel, he was unable at first to make himself believe he was in control of the boat. He groped consciously for a feeling of confidence that had to be instinctive to be any good at all. As he steered across the bay, he knew it wasn't right.

He did not start down the shore, but first turned north to haul the traps above Seal Bar. Although he found it difficult to steer a straight course through the choppy waves, he had no real trouble until he spotted the first buoy. He misjudged his approach and passed the buoy too far off to gaff it. He circled around and came to it again, and this time gauged the swing of the boat correctly.

He wanted to haul from the buoy on each trap to avoid trailing the warp over the side where a clumsy maneuver with the boat could catch it in the wheel. But on some of the traps this meant a lot of slack had to come in fast as the boat ran up over the trap. While he brought in the warp hand over hand as quickly as he could, usually to the first toggle and sometimes beyond, the boat

157

would begin to swing off in the rush of the windblown waves. Then he would have to reach the wheel to bring her into the wind again while holding the warp in one hand. Too often he found he ended up hauling against himself, not coming up over the trap the way he should as he hauled the warp on the winch head.

And then there were the other buoys—the Tates', Canada's and those belonging to the other lobstermen. As he took the lobsters from each trap, threw out the crabs and baited up, he had to run the boat through the maze of gear around him, being careful not to work in too close to the foaming rocks, and mindful not to reset the trap too far out, off the good bottom.

Sunlight came and went as the streaking clouds moved above him. In the noise of the engine and the wind and the tumbling waves, within the hissing spray and the graceless pitching of the boat, he lost his fear.

Finally he hauled a trap exactly right, and as he worked his way toward North Head, he began to feel more in place, more a part of the boat. He hauled the traps on Patience Shoal, then headed back for Tragedy Bluff. He thought the wind was gusting higher than before and backing around to blow from the north. The chop was very confused, and again as he came down the shore toward the bluff, the swells rolling in from the south and southeast added to the turmoil of the gray, tormented water.

While he was hauling off the bluff, he saw the *Pretty Lady* suddenly appear below Hundred Wreck Ledges. When she dipped into the trough, she was nearly hidden by the clouds of spray flying above the rocks. The tide was still ebbing; Petey went down on each string and hauled back. The Tates were hauling directly up the shore toward him.

He was drenched to his skin by now despite his oilskins. They were full of holes anyway, and he felt as though a ton of water had found its way through each separate tear. He was feeling the strain of trying to do everything. Running the boat and hauling and clearing the traps and baiting, he had no time to plug or even measure all the lobsters. He put the doubtful ones into a separate basket, and when he reached the shelter of one of the small coves above the Ledges, he paused long enough to catch up and gulp a cup of hot coffee.

It was the first moment he had had to take stock of his chances to go on hauling the rest of the way. From the occasional glimpses he had of the sun, he knew it was already late morning. Time was racing like the clouds overhead. Soon the tide would turn and begin to run against the wind, driving the waves higher. The farther he went down the shore, the farther from home he would be if he ran into trouble. And still the wind was rising.

He tried to eat a sandwich, but after two mouthfuls he couldn't swallow any more. Beside him the engine idled smoothly, but he remembered rough days before when she had sucked dirt into her carburetor and nearly stalled. He wasn't sure he would be able to coax her out of a bad spell the way Granddad could.

He looked out over the water and knew he shouldn't have stopped. He was afraid again.

The barrel of shedders was nearly full. He wasn't doing so well with the barrel of hard ones, but he had the best traps left. He couldn't quit now, even with the fear. The Tates were hauling too. As long as they were out, working for the money to buy the *Wild Wind*, he would not go in. He could think of no other reason for them to be out today.

"Petey!"

He turned and saw Granddad standing on the gravel beach. The sight of him started Petey moving. He threw overboard the buoy he had used to hold the *Jenny and Susan* behind the sheltering arm of the cove and went out to face the sea again.

He passed close to the *Pretty Lady* on the way to his next trap. The Tates watched him go by, then circled around him as he hauled. Several times they cut across his bow and forced him to swing away to avoid a collision. Because of this he set one trap nearly on top of another.

"Where's Gramps?" Spider yelled.

Petey gaffed his next buoy. As he pulled in the slack, he watched Spider jump to his wheel. Both boats rolled in the chop dangerously close to each other.

"Better go in, kid," Spider bellowed. "You could get hurt out here."

Petey swung the *Jenny and Susan* to starboard as he held the turns on the winch head. "Move off before you wreck us both!"

Spider looked back over his stern at Petey. "We're going to buy your father's boat tomorrow. How's that strike you?"

Petey took out two shedders from the trap he pulled onto the washboard and held them up to show Spider. "Long as I get traps like this you'll never have a chance to buy the *Wild Wind.*"

"Deven's going to sell her to us," Spider shouted. Danny bobbed his head up and down.

"Not till noon tomorrow, he's not." Petey quickly baited the trap and ran up the shore a short distance before setting it back in the water. Spider brought the *Pretty Lady* in close beside him again.

"What if you wasn't to live till tomorrow?" Spider shouted at him. "I guess we'd get the *Wild Wind* then."

Petey stared across the foaming water at him. The wind blew spray into his face. "You figure to do something to me?"

Spider threw back his head and laughed. "On a day like this something might just happen to you, like an accident."

Petey couldn't tell how serious he was, but he didn't like the eager, mad look on Danny's face. Spider was still laughing as the two boats drew apart.

From then on he was never without them. Steering far outside the surf pounding on Hundred Wreck Ledges, Petey ran down the shore to the traps below. The *Pretty Lady* followed him.

The wind was out of the north now, raking down the shore beneath a dark-blue, purple-clouded sky. There was no warmth from the sun when it came out, only the cold salt sting of the tearing wind. After low water slack, the tide began running up the shore against the wind, and the chop rose high and sharp-backed.

Below the Tates' cove Petey broke both toggles on

one warp and had to reach under the stern for an extra bottle while the boat circled untended, rolling badly before he could get back to the wheel. Odd thoughts flashed through his mind as he struggled to haul—laughing taunts from Leo, hard words from Granddad, something Dad had told him years ago that he couldn't remember clearly now. Every so often he would see Sheila's face and feel an ache inside him that wasn't fear but something like it, a sense of loss he could not account for.

A turn caught on the winch head, and he had to pull hard to free the warp. Above the Cut, he circled twice trying to free a trap that was caught down, but had to give up for fear of parting it off.

He saw Granddad watching him from a high point of land farther down the shore. Petey waved, but Granddad stood without moving, his shirt flapping in the wind.

The Tates were hauling close by, their own boat heavily rolling whenever she came broadside to the sharp waves.

He was rounding off a crate with shedders now. Hard lobsters were scarce even down here, and hauling all the traps inshore wasn't going to be enough. To get a good start on a second crate of shedders and fill the barrel of hard ones, he would have to haul the pairs on the Triangle Ground, for they had set over an extra night.

Below the Cut, the shore curved around more and more to the west, and he was no longer exposed to the full force of the wind as he hauled. This made him all the more reluctant to head out for the Triangle Ground. He had been lucky so far—all his mistakes had been small ones.

If he hadn't gained confidence handling the *Jenny and Susan* all through the day, he would have stopped with his last trap inshore and gone down around to sell. But he felt right at the wheel now; he felt he could go out to the Triangle Ground and get the hundred pounds of lobsters he still needed.

And so he went out toward open water, toward Triangle Rock at the edge of the windblown clouds. He stood at the wheel looking back and saw the *Pretty Lady* turn near Lost Shoal and follow. He remembered Spider's threatening words. He had never until now felt so alone and when he thought of Sheila again, that same strange sense of loss swept over him, even stronger than before.

Stern to the wind the *Jenny and Susan* dipped and surged on her way out to the Triangle Ground. Petey tried again to eat some of the food Gram had packed in the dinner pail, but although he felt lightheaded from hunger, he could force little down. The coffee was gone by now, and his mouth stayed dry.

The Tates were trying to overtake him. For most of the way they gained only slowly, but he had to cut his speed as the waves steepened, and the Tates plunged recklessly ahead. They were passing a bottle back and forth where they stood at the wheel, and as they went by him, Danny held the bottle out in Petey's direction. Petey could see them laughing, but all he could hear was the pounding of the Buick beside him. He wondered if the whisky really made it better, or if the fear was still there, under the silliness and false bravery.

The surf breaking on the ledges around Triangle Rock was smashing all the way into the shore of the tiny island. Petey swung off long before he came close. The change in course brought the wind and water more onto his starboard side. He braced himself by the wheel and wondered how he could possibly stay on his feet when he started to haul.

On the open water the wind was blowing harder than it had inshore all day. It roared down from the north—from the distant, out of sight mainland—driving the high, sharp waves before it. Petey gripped the wheel as if it was the only safety he had. The sky was completely overcast again, the clouds dark gray with tattered streamers torn from below. He saw the *Pretty Lady* dip far down between the waves as he stared ahead, looking for the first of Granddad's buoys.

In the gray, white-foaming water he was almost upon one of the buoys before he saw it. He swung toward it, took a sea against the starboard side, then grabbed up the gaff too late. On the second pass he came too fast and close, and after gaffing the buoy, he quickly pushed in the clutch to keep the warp from fouling the wheel while he pulled in the slack. He tried to lay the buoy and toggles so that they would go out automatically when he reset the pair, but nothing would stay put on the stern deck.

There were five big counters in the pair of traps, and he went on to the next with high hopes. With each pair he hauled he told himself he was that much nearer to the end, that much closer to being home free. But the constant plunging of the boat while the windblown spray splashed over him was wearing his courage thin. His hands trembled as he filled the bait needle. For a moment he stopped breathing when the engine caught, sputtered, and almost stalled. He nursed her along until she was running smoothly again, then circled back for the pair he had missed. He could feel panic edging through him.

Six pairs, seven, eight, nine, ten. He was putting his shedders into the second crate. The proportion of hard lobsters was higher out here, but the barrel he was putting them in was still not full. He had enough traps left, with luck. . . .

He hauled two pairs for only snappers, but the next pair was the best of the day with three counters in the main trap and eight in the second, plus a couple he put in the doubtful basket. As he worked toward the southern edge of the Triangle Ground, he began to think he was going to make his haul.

Hauling pairs was especially difficult alone. When the main trap came up, he had to take the turns from the winch head, then get some slack on the warp to the second trap while pulling the main trap up onto the washboard. Once he had the second warp on the winch, he could reach the wheel again.

Fifteen pairs, sixteen, seventeen . . . twenty. He wasn't sure of his count, but he knew there were only ten or eleven pairs left. He had to have the second crate as nearly full as possible. He couldn't go through all this to lose out by a few pounds.

The Tates were hauling above him. Occasionally he saw them as he turned, but he could not, for more than a few seconds, take his eyes off his work. The bait was nearly gone; he was stretching it out as much as he could. He broke another toggle, cut his hand on a sliver of glass that had stuck into the warp. Blood ran down his fingers and dripped to the platform.

He hauled on, so tired he couldn't get the crabs out fast enough. He left most of them in now. He had to finish and get in before he blundered into trouble. Twenty-four pairs, twenty-five, twenty-six . . .

He had the next to last pair of traps on the washboard when he saw the *Pretty Lady* cutting his way, her bow driving deep into the water as she plunged down the sloping seas. He glanced at her again while he was putting two hard counters into the barrel. Spider was coming directly toward him.

Petey baited the two traps and tied the doors shut. The second crate of shedders was only half full, but if fifteen or twenty of the lobsters in the doubtful basket went the measure, he would have enough. The last pair could make it a sure thing. . . .

He was ready to circle around and set when he realized the Tates were only a few yards off his starboard side. Not daring to ignore them any longer, he hurried forward to the wheel, his heart racing. As the *Jenny and Susan* surged ahead, he looked around and saw that the Tates were still gaining. The *Pretty Lady* rolled her side down no more than ten feet away.

Petey could see Spider laughing at him. It began to sink in that this was Spider's move, that he meant to kill him. Out here there was no one to see what went on, no one to say later that anything more than an accident had happened.

He swung off to avoid a collision, hanging onto the wheel as a sea rolled under the *Jenny and Susan*'s stern. By now they were off the Triangle Ground, plunging south with the seas following.

Danny was leering at him from the stern of the *Pretty Lady*, staggering about recklessly, apparently too drunk to care how near he came to falling overboard. Spider was edging closer. The two boats almost touched as they both yawed off course. Petey couldn't turn to starboard with the Tates so close. He'd have to turn the other way to make a run for Hunter Island.

He darted back to pull the traps in off the washboard but slid on the wet platform and fell. As he scrambled up, he saw Spider throw something. It was too late for him to regain the shelter of the deckhouse. Instinctively he ducked his head as a ballast rock slammed into his right shoulder. He lost his balance again and fell hard on his side into the loosely coiled warp near the stern.

He could feel the boat tilting under him as she yawed to one side and then the other. She rose up wildly, then came down veering to starboard. The two boats came together with an impact that shook the *Jenny and Susan* her whole length. Another rock struck him on the back of his neck. He had to get to the wheel, but it seemed a long way above him. He tried to clear his mind. Panic clawed through him as he felt something tighten like wire around his left thigh. He was being pulled toward the side and as he tried to stop himself with his hands, he looked up and saw that the traps were gone. The *Jenny and Susan* had pitched them overboard, and tangled in the warp, he was being dragged after them.

TWENTY

~~~~~~

Left to Die

He was able to wedge himself under the stern deck in the angle it formed with the washboard. The drag from the pair of traps had drawn the warp so tightly around his left leg that there was no way he could slip free. Throbbing pain beat through his leg. He didn't dare try to stand, for fear he would be pulled into the water. If he stayed where he was . . .

The *Jenny and Susan* was yawing widely as she ran before the following sea. With each surge against her stern she rolled more of her starboard side under. He had to get to the wheel, but as long as she was driving ahead as fast as she was, he couldn't free himself from the warp.

The knife . . . He could see the bait knife stuck into the wall of the deckhouse. It might as well be a hundred miles away. . . . The warp was cutting into his leg. Reaching up over the stern deck coaming, he tried to pull back on the warp to get some slack, but his twisted position prevented him from using his strength. He fell back, knowing this was hopeless. Turning, he stared at the wheel through a red mist, blinked and tried to focus his

168

eyes on the platform around him. He was looking for something, a piece of glass, anything he could use to cut the warp. . . . As the boat rolled, his stomach tightened. The *Jenny and Susan* put her washboard under, and water spilled over the coaming.

She was going to fill and he was as good as dead, unless he could cut himself out of the warp. Only then did he think of the spare toggles under the stern. Were there any left? He tried to think but couldn't remember. He twisted around and reached as far as he could. His fingers just brushed against the small basket that held the bottles.

He swore at himself to hurry. The boat was swinging more and more into the trough, nearly broadside now to the seas and that damned wind that was a gale out here and wanted to kill him—to finish the killing that the Tates had begun.

With all his strength he forced himself farther under the stern. His fingers gripped the edge of the basket, and he pulled it closer to him. His hand searched the emptiness inside. Wildly now he tipped the basket over and the last bottle fell against his arm. Clutching it tightly, he inched his way out into the open.

The pain from his leg was all through him now, burning into his stomach and back. Water poured over the coaming, choking him, stinging his eyes. He smashed the bottle against the stern and used the jagged end in his hand to slash at the warp taut-pulling from his leg. Before he had cut it through, it parted from the tension, and he fell back rolling as the platform tilted steeply. He scrambled onto his feet, fell, threw himself forward toward the wheel. He couldn't stand on his leg, so he crawled.

Pulling himself up to the wheel, he saw a wall of water sweeping toward him. He swung the bow around to meet the wave, bracing himself with one hand on the roof of the deckhouse and most of his weight on his good leg. The *Jenny and Susan* rose to the sea, took it, plunged through and over, drove her bow down toward the next sea coming.

Petey cut back his speed until it felt right. Strength was returning to his left leg now, and he widened his stance by the wheel as the boat drove ahead to the north. He couldn't see the *Pretty Lady* anywhere. The Tates had left him to die, but he hadn't; he was coming back alive.

He wondered how badly the *Pretty Lady* had been damaged when the two boats struck. The *Jenny and Susan* seemed to have stood it well. She might be leaking, but she had taken so much water over her sides today that he couldn't tell for sure. He could see the dark bilge water below the engine. There was no chance to pump it out now, but he checked regularly to see if it was rising.

Far ahead he saw Triangle Rock above the torn sea. He shifted course a little to give the island a wide berth. He realized now that he had forgotten to pour the extra five gallons of gas into the tank before coming out to the Triangle Ground. With all the extra running he had done, he would be lucky to get back to Hunter Island before the tank went dry.

He glanced back and saw that the lobster barrels had

shifted toward the stern but were in no danger of tipping over. He had a full barrel and full crate of shedders plus the other crate half filled. The barrel of hard lobsters was nearly up to the rim. Everything depended on how many of the questionable lobsters in the basket he would have to throw away.

He was alive, he had saved himself, but it was all for nothing unless he had the lobsters he needed.

The rest of the way in, he stood tensely by the wheel holding the boat into the wind and waves, listening for the gas to run out. As soon as he could, he turned off more toward the west. In the sheltered water under the lee of Hunter Island he went to the stern for the five-gallon can. He quickly emptied the gasoline into the tank, then returned to the wheel. All afternoon death had been with him on board the *Jenny and Susan*. He forced away the exhausted remnants of his fear. He still had to sell and get home.

There was little wind in close to the shore with the whole sheltering mass of the island on his starboard side. He could see the clouds breaking up before the high gale above the island, and occasionally he tasted the chill, raw flavor of a swirling gust, but the *Jenny and Susan* cruised easily along the smooth, empty channel between the ledges and the shore.

He went forward to put on the belt to the bilge pump. The belt that drove the winch had whipped off during his attempt to escape the Tates and was lying half in the greasy water below the engine. He pulled it clear, then hurried back to the wheel. He would know soon enough if hitting the *Pretty Lady* had opened up any seams.

He pulled the basket of lobsters closer to the wheel and began measuring them, throwing the short ones over the side and putting the counters into the second crate or into the barrel if they were hard ones. He didn't cheat; all the snappers went back into the water. When he was done, he gave the second crate a long look.

"Maybe," he said out loud. He closed the top and put away the brass measure.

It was late afternoon, and when the sun broke through, it was low in the western sky and without warmth. He thought the wind was backing into the northwest. He hoped it was, for this would give him an easier trip up the shore after he sold.

He was growing stiff standing by the wheel in his cold, wet clothes. His shoulder and his neck ached. He tried to rub away the tightness in his left leg but the muscles stayed hard as iron all the way to town.

He had thought he would see Granddad on one of the beaches or headlands of rock along the shore. But if he was somewhere watching, he was well hidden. He might be waiting in town, although Petey doubted he would make a scene in front of Carl Julian or anyone else. Petey had no real idea what Granddad was going to do when he came in. He wasn't looking forward to finding out.

The Tates came roaring out of the harbor as he rode in, and when the two boats passed each other no more than ten yards apart, he saw the shocked look on both their faces.

"Sobers you up, doesn't it," he shouted at them.

Danny was still staring at him when Petey cut in toward Carl Julian's lobster car. He tied up and gave a shout, and Julian came out on the wharf.

"Sure didn't expect to see any of you eastsiders today," he said as he crossed the car. "Then in come the Tates and then you two. Blowing some, wasn't it?"

Petey nodded. "Some." He rolled one barrel over and lifted it up to Julian. "Hard ones. Rest are shedders."

"Had quite a haul, didn't you?" Julian leaned down and looked into the bow of the boat. "Hey, where's Will?"

"He didn't haul today." Petey lifted the other barrel onto the washboard.

"What do you mean he didn't haul today?"

"He didn't."

"Is he sick?"

"No."

"Petey, you mean he let you haul all by yourself on a day like this?"

Petey looked up at him but didn't answer his question. "I'll help you plug these if you want. I didn't have time while I was hauling."

Julian stared at him. Petey turned his back and dragged the two crates over. He wasn't going to explain anything to Julian or anyone else. It was between him and Granddad.

While Julian was weighing the lobsters, Petey straightened out the mess on board. He coiled up the warp left from the lost pair and threw it with the buoy under the stern. The bilge pump had stopped pumping. He kicked off the belt before looking down under the engine.

174 The Winds of Summer

There seemed to be just the usual trickle of water drain-
ing forward from the stern.

He leaned out over the starboard side. Except for a
place where the paint was scraped, the only damage
from hitting the *Pretty Lady* was a section of splintered
guardrail. It didn't look very good, but it would be easy
to replace.

"Something wrong?" Carl Julian asked from behind
him.

"Nothing much," Petey said. "Want to plug those lobsters?"

Julian grinned at him. "Quite a man, ain't you? Talka-
tive as a clam."

Petey would have liked to smile. "I'm too tired to
talk."

When he was ready to go with the brim salted down
in the bait barrels, Julian handed him the slip with his
money. Petey glanced at the figures written on the slip.
He had brought in seventy-five pounds of hard lobsters
and two hundred and forty-seven pounds of shedders. At
eighty and sixty cents it came out to two hundred and
eight dollars and change. His bait had already taken ten
dollars away from this.

He thanked Julian and went on to Mel Swift's for gas
and oil. His heart was beating hard, but he forced himself
to tend seriously to the business of gassing up. He filled
the tank and the extra can and bought three quarts of oil,
and when he had paid there was one hundred and
eighty-five dollars left. The half of this he had earned by

hauling alone would give him the ninety dollars he needed to complete his savings for the *Wild Wind.*

On his way through the harbor he added it up again, but he had won, there was no question of it. He turned to look at the *Wild Wind* on her mooring, then on an impulse he circled back and went around her twice. He waved his arms at her and started to laugh, and the laughter felt like sandbags falling from his shoulders. He let out a hoot loud enough to be heard all over the harbor, but he didn't care who knew how happy he was, and he circled the *Wild Wind* one more time before he headed out.

He started washing down the boat, stepping to the wheel whenever he had to adjust the course. Groggy with tiredness, his leg throbbing, he was above all tasting a big victory for the first time in his life and he didn't want to let it go.

But there was still Granddad. He had not been at Carl Julian's. He was probably home. Stealing the boat had been wrong, and Petey knew Granddad would expect him to pay for it in some way.

He ran the boat up the east side toward the bay and Fox Cove. The wind was from the northwest now and moderating. Above the rough sea, the sky had cleared to a cold and distant blue. He guided the boat home to whatever was waiting for him.

TWENTY-ONE

~~~~~~

Facing Granddad

Gram was setting the kitchen table. She looked up at him as he came in. Her eyes were red. "Are you all right?" she asked. She continued to lay the silverware as she waited for his answer.

"Yes."

"You're soaked through. Go change before you catch cold."

"Where's Granddad?"

"There's plenty of time for that. Get into some dry clothes."

He knew she was trying to protect him, to delay what had to come anyway. "Where is he, Gram?"

"Why did you have to do it, Petey?" She rushed around the table and took his arms in her hands.

He tried to pull away. "You'll get the bait stink on you."

"Never mind that. You've caused such an upset. He's been beside himself all day, half the time wanting to get help, the rest of the time telling me you deserved to drown out there. As if he believed that! He tried to get Canada's boat, but his engine broke down two days ago and he's waiting for parts from the mainland."

She wouldn't let him go, but the longer he put off facing Granddad the worse it was going to be. "I made the money I need," he told her. "And I'm giving Granddad half what I cleared."

She stared at him as if he had suddenly spoken to her in Spanish.

"I've got the money for the *Wild Wind*."

"And how are you going to make up to him for what you've done?"

He shrugged.

"You're a wild, willful boy. Do you think he can just let this go by? He hasn't any choice, Petey."

"Where is he?"

She pushed him away. "In the shop. He's waiting for you in the shop."

He walked to the entry, but she called to him. "What's wrong with your leg? Why are you limping?"

"It's nothing."

"I prayed for you all day, Petey. Prayed you'd come back to us safe. And you're back."

The only light in the shop came through one dirty window. Petey closed the door and waited for his eyes to become used to the gloom, his heart beating rapidly.

"So you're back."

Petey walked toward the tool bench until he saw Granddad sitting on a crate behind the stove. "Yes sir."

"Did anything go wrong?"

"Not much. I lost a pair below the Triangle Ground.

And . . . and I hit the *Pretty Lady*. There wasn't much damage."

"How did you manage that?"

"Well . . ."

"Tell it straight. I'll listen."

Petey leaned back against the bench and told Granddad everything that had happened. When he was done, Granddad was silent for a long time.

"How badly are you hurt?" he asked.

"I'm all right. Just sore."

"The Tates tried to kill you."

"Yes sir."

"You were damned lucky."

"Yes sir."

"What's the matter? Are you crying?"

"No. It's just my nose."

"Well blow it!"

Petey took out his wet handkerchief. The shop was so dark he could barely see the outline of Granddad's face.

"You plan on reporting them Tates to Chief Coughlin?" Granddad asked.

"No sir."

"Why not?"

"Because I don't have any proof of what happened, and besides . . ."

"You brought it on yourself," Granddad finished for him.

"That wasn't what I was going to say."

"But you did bring it on yourself. If you had drowned out there it would have been your own fault. Do you understand that?"

Petey nodded.

"Do you?"

"Yes sir."

"If you had wrecked my boat, the same thing. Your fault. Right?"

"Yes."

"Can't you say anything more than that?" Granddad's voice came louder now, with a harsh, cutting force to the words.

"I knew the chance I was taking." Petey pulled out his wallet and placed Granddad's share on the bench. "That's your half. I've got the money I need for the *Wild Wind* now."

"That's real good, Petey. But why don't you come over here and give me my half? You afraid of me?"

Petey put the slips with the folded bills and walked over to where Granddad was sitting. "Here."

Granddad's large, dry hand closed over his, pressing his fingers tightly against the money. The pain took Petey's breath away.

"Are you man enough to take that?" Granddad demanded,

"Yes sir."

Granddad pried the money free and released his hand. "You think you're my equal now, do you?" he asked. "You took my boat, you disobeyed me, you risked my only means of making a living. You must think you're more of a man than I am."

"No I don't."

Granddad stood up. For the first time Petey saw the leather belt in his left hand, and he stepped back.

"Stay where you are!"

"I'm not going to let you beat me with that."

"I'll tell you something, boy. I was down on Lookout Beach when you came in from the Triangle Ground. I saw you coming and . . ." Granddad stopped.

"I didn't see you."

"Once I knew you were in all right, I drove back here. Didn't want no fuss in town. Ain't no one's damn business except ours. But all the way home I kept asking myself what I was going to do. Because I was proud of you, because you'll make a fine man someday, but you did wrong, boy, you did wrong."

Petey waited for him to go on. Granddad stepped toward him, swinging the belt into his right hand.

"I want you to tell me that what you did was wrong!" Granddad shouted. "I want you to tell me you're sorry."

"I'm sorry I took your boat. I'm sorry I made you and Gram worry. But I'm not sorry I went out and hauled for the money I needed. I'm not going to lie to you, Granddad."

"That's not enough, Petey. I've got to beat the wildness out of you the way I should have beat it out of your father. Maybe he'd be alive today if I had."

Petey pulled back, but the belt caught him hard on his ribs. He staggered against the bench, tried to duck away toward the door. The end of the belt hit the corner of his mouth. He tasted blood. He reached out blindly to ward off the next swing. The belt lashed around his arm, and he managed to grab it with his right hand. He pulled himself up straight, hanging onto the belt with all his strength.

"I won't let you, Granddad!"

"You're too much like your father."

"I won't let you."

"Petey!"

They both pulled on the belt, but neither would let go. Finally Granddad shoved him away with his foot, snapping the belt free as Petey fell over a pile of laths.

Granddad was swinging the belt behind him again, ready to bring it down. Petey came up fast to defend himself. They faced each other across the clutter of the shop. The dim evening light glowing in the window seemed only to make the shadows darker. Slowly, ever so slowly, Granddad lowered his arm. He cursed softly.

"You're your father all over again. You keep on this way, you'll die like him too. But I can't beat you, I can't change you, no more than I could beat him, change him. Maybe it's a mistake, you living here with us."

These last words frightened Petey far more than the belt. "We still need each other, Granddad," he said. "We really do."

Granddad walked over to the chopping block and sat down.

"Granddad?" Petey waited in the dark silence. "Don't we?"

There was no answer. A sob tore up through Petey's chest. He turned and ran outside.

After supper Petey went to the old house to tell Leo he'd be riding down with him in the morning to pay Mr. Deven for the *Wild Wind*.

Leo nodded over his beer. "I'll drive in and pick you up when I'm ready. Don't want you down here at six o'clock pounding on my door."

Petey spent a restless night trying to sleep. Through

his window he could hear the wind in the spruce trees, but later, in the dark middle of the night when he woke up from the ache in his leg, there was only the distant sound of breaking waves outside the bay to edge the stillness. Granddad had driven off alone in his car shortly after Petey came home from Leo's. Petey wondered if he was back at the house now. More than this he wondered where he had gone and what was on his mind.

In the morning he was awake early, but he waited for them to get up. He dressed and sat on the edge of his bed looking out the window at the cove in the bright sunlight. The sky was as blue as he had ever seen it.

He walked out into the hall when they went downstairs. The wind had risen again. It wasn't blowing as hard as yesterday, but it moaned steadily around the eaves of the house. He went downstairs stiffly, still favoring his left leg.

Over breakfast Granddad began to speak. "Last night I went to town to call your mother," he told Petey. He cut his piece of fried ham in half. "I was going to have her meet you in Grant Harbor. I was figuring not to have you stay here with us any longer."

Petey dumped sugar into his coffee.

"But I didn't call her."

Petey met his look and started to ask why. Granddad silenced him.

"I'm not through talking," he snapped. "We have to come to an understanding. Otherwise we can't go on living together. Yesterday we both went too far. But what you said about us still needing each other is true."

Petey picked up his cup in both hands and brought it

to his mouth. The smell of the coffee was strong and good. He breathed deeply. Granddad was staring at Gram.

"We need you around here, Petey." Granddad tapped the table with his fingers. "You work hard, you're strong, you're good with your hands and your mind. And I guess you still need us, even if you are trying to grow up in one big jump. Because you haven't made it yet."

Petey heard Leo's truck coming into the dooryard.

"But there are some conditions you'll have to agree to, Petey."

"What conditions?"

"First off, you'll have to build me a pair of traps to replace the pair you lost, and buy me the warp to set them."

"Yes sir."

Granddad reached for his pipe and filled it. "Then there's what you did to the *Jenny and Susan*. I went down to check her last night. You'll help me fix the damage and pay for what we need."

"Yes sir."

"Now I'm not going to stop you from setting your own string of traps and hauling on your own. I guess if you didn't drown yesterday, you can take care of yourself. But I'm not going to help you, not even with one old trap. Buy your own trap stock, build them up yourself, buy your own warp to set them. I'm not going to give you a thing. If you have to go in debt, that's your business, but I won't back you, not for so much as a pound of three-pennies. Understand?"

Petey nodded.

"Will," Gram said.

"You stay out of this, woman. It's between me and Petey."

Leo was hitting his horn outside. Petey stood up, but Granddad reached over and pushed him back into his chair. "There's one more thing," he said. "While you're building up your string, you're perfectly welcome to haul with me whatever days you're not in school. You can make some money for your gear that way. But once you set out on your own, your board goes up to ten dollars a week."

Petey made a face.

"Never mind. That's the only way it can be. Agreed?"

"Yes sir."

"You keep your side of the bargain, and we'll keep ours. Otherwise you'll be off to your mother's before you know what's happened to you."

The side door opened, and Leo came through the entry. "Aren't you ready yet, Petey? Here I get up early to take you to town and then I've got to wait around."

"Sorry," Petey said. "Be right with you."

"You've got plenty of time," Granddad said. "Sit down and have a cup of coffee with us."

Petey was surprised, and Leo seemed uncertain of the invitation. He hung back near the entry.

Granddad cleared his throat. "I'm asking you to join us for a cup of coffee."

Without a word Leo walked across the kitchen and sat down. Gram poured fresh coffee all around. It was almost like old times.

TWENTY-TWO

~~~~~~

The Dream Alive

When Petey had gone upstairs for his money jar and they were ready to go, Granddad walked outside with them. "Are you going to bring the *Wild Wind* up around today? It's still rough out there."

Petey checked the movement of the trees in the wind. "Won't be anything like yesterday. I guess I'll bring her up."

Granddad nodded. "Make her fast to the stern of my boat. We'll have to see what we can do with that old mooring of your father's."

Petey and Leo climbed into the truck and started for town. As they bounced over the dirt road, Petey felt a warm happiness. Granddad's conditions for his staying were hard but fair. He could still have a small string built up and set before winter. And next year would be his. . . .

They found Mr. Deven's car parked in the driveway beside his funeral parlor. When he didn't answer their knock, Petey pushed open the door.

"Let's go in."

Leo shrugged but went with him through a short hall-way to the front room.

"Creepy," Petey said. He faintly remembered the room from when Dad had died—the velvet-cushioned chairs, the deep rug, the dark wallpaper. The sadness of the room was overwhelming. Light from outside barely penetrated the heavy drapes that were pulled across the windows.

"Makes you wonder," Leo said in a low voice.

"What?"

"Why people should live poor and die fancy."

"You hear something?"

Leo tilted his head toward the stairs at the other side of the room. "Yeah, someone's singing."

They crossed to the staircase and went up, Petey carrying the pickle jar full of money under his arm. On the second floor the singing was louder. They walked along a red-carpeted hallway to an open doorway in the back. Mr. Deven was bent over a coffin of dark hardwood, polishing it with a cloth. As they came in, he stopped singing.

"How did you get up here?" he demanded.

"You didn't hear us knocking," Petey told him. "The door was open." He looked around at the large display room. In addition to coffins of different woods there were several models of cement vaults.

Mr. Deven walked over to where they stood. "Is that the money?"

Petey nodded. "Four hundred and eighty dollars." He handed the money jar to the undertaker. "Better count it."

Deven walked around a coffin into a curtained alcove. "Do you have the receipt for the down payment?"

Petey ducked through the curtain. The undertaker was sitting at a desk under a fluorescent light. Petey took out his wallet and dropped the receipt next to the jar. "I know you're disappointed."

"Disappointed? Why should I be?" Mr. Deven opened the jar and began counting the bills.

"Because you didn't think I could make the money in time, and now you won't be able to get six hundred dollars from the Tates."

Deven went on counting. "Surprised, even a bit regretful, Petey. But not disappointed."

Petey knew he was lying, putting on a big show the way he had when Dad died. He shifted uneasily from one foot to the other. The air in the little office was choking him. "Okay if I look around?"

"Go ahead."

Petey rejoined Leo in the display room. Together they looked at each of the coffins. By the time they reached the last one, Leo was shaking his head. "I'm going to be cremated."

"That's a most inconvenient arrangement," Mr. Deven said as he walked toward them across the soundless rug.

"Inconvenient for who?" Leo asked.

Deven seemed shocked. "For those you leave behind, of course."

Leo grinned. "I'm not too worried about them."

Deven handed Petey a folded sheet of paper. "Here's your bill of sale."

Petey opened it and read it carefully. Then he handed it to Leo who scanned down the sheet and nodded.

188 The Winds of Summer

"She's all yours now, Petey," Leo said. "How's it feel?"

Suddenly the deadliness of the room, of the whole funeral parlor was too much for him. He grabbed the bill of sale from Leo. "Let's go."

He ran out into the hall and down the stairs. He hardly saw the front room as he charged through it on his way to the door. By the time he reached the truck, his legs were trembling. He longed to be out in his boat away from Mr. Deven and his kind of death, away from the land and all the land people, away from everyone except . . .

Leo was walking toward him.

"Hey," Petey said. "Let's pick up Sheila. I want to take her with me when I go up around in the boat."

He saw Sheila wearing a blue shirt and jeans walking barefoot along the dirt road with a bag of groceries in her arms. Before Leo could slide the truck to a stop on the hard dirt, Petey had jumped out and tumbled past her into the bushes beside the road.

"Petey! Are you all right?"

He picked himself up, grinning at her surprised look. "I'm fine. Come on out with me."

"In the truck?"

"In my boat."

"Petey, did you really . . ."

"The *Wild Wind*'s mine. Got the bill of sale in my wallet." He scrambled up the shoulder of the road and tried to hug her. She pushed the bag of groceries into his arms instead.

"I have to bring these home first, Petey," she said. "Barbie has a wicked hangover."

Leo had backed up to where they were standing. Petey handed him the groceries, then helped Sheila up onto the seat. On the ride to her house, she asked him a dozen questions. He told her part of the story but left out what had happened on the Triangle Ground. It wasn't that he didn't want to impress her. He did. But not with Leo there, all ready to start laughing out of the side of his mouth.

At her house he carried in the groceries and waited for her to get her scarf. "Better bring a sweater too," he yelled, without thinking. "You'll be cold out there."

Barbie gave him an ugly look. She was standing at the table searching through the groceries. "Do you have to shout? She can't hear you."

"Sorry."

"Might have some consideration," she grumbled as she walked to the refrigerator.

Petey made a face at her back. Sheila came in, saw him and laughed.

Barbie turned around with a bottle of vodka in her hand. She slammed the refrigerator door. "I thought I asked you to get tomato juice."

"They didn't have any," Sheila told her. "Look, Barb, I'm going with Petey. I'll help you straighten out when I get home."

"Fine, go off and leave me with this mess staring at me all day."

"Well, I didn't make it. You and Ruth did." Sheila's face flushed a pretty pink. "I'm ready, Petey."

They ran out to the truck and climbed into the cab. As they drove back onto the road, Sheila tied her scarf over her hair. "They make me so mad. If they didn't have me around, that place would really look like a barn."

"Forget them," Petey told her. "Forget everyone."

She smiled at him. "I'm glad you're happy."

Leo took them down to Mr. Deven's wharf. Petey wanted him to come along on the ride up the east side, but Leo shook his head.

"I'd only get sick, rough as it is. I'll meet you at the cove. Here, take a couple of extra dollars for gas."

He stood on the wharf watching them row out to the *Wild Wind* in Mr. Deven's punt. Petey turned once to wave back at him. By the time they were off the mooring and gliding in toward Mel Swift's float, he was gone.

"I think he really wanted to come," Sheila said.

Petey nodded.

He had four dollars' worth of gas put in the tank. When he came back from paying, Sheila was sitting on the stern deck. He cast off the line and started for the harbor mouth. On the way out he took the *Wild Wind* close to Carl Julian's lobster car. Julian looked up from a crate and waved his cap.

Beyond the inside ledges Petey opened the throttle and the *Wild Wind* put down her stern. He looked back and saw Sheila watching him. He motioned her to come stand beside him, but she shook her head. For a while after that he was conscious of her there behind him, but later, as they left the narrows inside Mussel Island for the more open water beyond, he forgot her in his excitement.

He studied the sea ahead, then stepped back from under the deckhouse roof to look around at the sky. All the offshore islands stood out in perfect sharp-edged detail. Far out he could see the white-capped chop, and now the wind began to dip down in gusts full of the smell of fall. He looked forward to the rough water on the east side. He wanted the *Wild Wind* to charge the chop, to rise and fall beneath his feet. He wanted her fully alive to match the fullness inside him.

He felt much more than happiness. He could almost hear Dad's voice in the steady beat of the engine, almost sense his guidance at the wheel. This, Dad's boat, was his own now, but for as long into the future as he worked her up and down the shore, for as long as he ran her under blue or gray skies, over smooth or angry water, Dad would be there on board her too.

Time seemed to disappear as he ran the boat toward the east side. There was only the timeless day—the sun that would set and rise again and always be there and the sea that pulsed with the tides, moved with the wind and yet never changed at all. Once through the channel between the rocks and Broad Ledge, he followed the shore as it curved around to the north. The *Wild Wind* came alive for him as he had dreamed she would.

He leaned outside the deckhouse and watched the way the bow took the chop, then looked to the stern at Sheila watching him. There was a smile on her lips, and it broadened as he stared at her. He returned to the wheel, and this time she came forward to be with him and he let her steer a while.

Inside Lost Shoal he took the wheel again. As they passed Bottomless Cove and the Cut, he could see spray flying over Hundred Wreck Ledges. He took them well outside. Even so, Sheila was a little frightened. She held onto his arm as the boat pitched through the rough water above the Ledges. Her hair brushed his face in spite of her scarf, and he pulled it off to let her hair blow free.

"Petey!"

"Never mind."

He steered for Tragedy Bluff and finally they could see East Bay opening up before them—Seal Bar, Parsons Ledge, then Rocky Point as they cleared the bluff and headed in. He sent the boat on at full speed now and watched the shore line of the cove grow larger. He could see Granddad and Gram and Leo waving to them from the rocks of the point. They were all there and Sheila was with him and he was bringing the *Wild Wind* home.